Darby brushed the beads of moisture from her eye-lashes and followed the filly's stare, but she didn't spot anything worth Hoku's attention.

"What do you see, girl?" Darby asked.

Mist obscured the spot where the road came to an end and rolling hills began. She could picture the grassland ahead.

"Ow!"

The lead rope jerked tight around Darby's hand. Bones grated against each other.

Amputation, Darby thought, but the lead rope slipped free of her hand as Hoku bolted.

Playful as a colt, the sorrel tossed her nose in the direction of something only she could see, and gave a half buck.

An invitation to kick up your heels, Darby thought, hunting for the creature Hoku was greeting. *Whoever you are, please don't accept!*

There. A black-and-white form emerged from the mist and resolved itself into a beautiful paint horse.

Check out the

Phantom Stallion

series, also by Terri Farley!

Read all of Darby's adventures!

Phantom Stallion
WILD HORSE ISLAND

Phantom Stallion

WILD HORSE ISLAND 7

MISTWALKER

TERRI FARLEY

HarperTrophy®
An Imprint of HarperCollinsPublishers

Harper Trophy® is a registered trademark
of HarperCollins Publishers.

Mistwalker

Copyright © 2008 by Terri Sprenger-Farley

Library of Congress Catalog Card Number: 2007934248
ISBN 978-0-06-088620-2

❖

First Harper Trophy edition, 2008

This book is dedicated to Mervina Cash-Kaeo, Esq., whose explanation of *ho'oponopono* over a great Hawaiian breakfast inspired the salvation of more than one relationship; to Dr. Janet Six who introduced me to the rain-forest ruins of Hawaiian sugar plantations; and to Lisa Harper for emergency medical knowledge and an uncanny ability to enter my world of "what if?"

© Gary Chalk

TWO SISTERS VOLCANOES

MESSAGE
BOTTLE LANDING

'IOLANI
RANCH

RAIN
FOREST

SUN
HOUSE

OLD PLANTATION

TUTU'S
COTTAGE

CRIMSON
VALE

NIGHT DIGGER
POINT BEACH

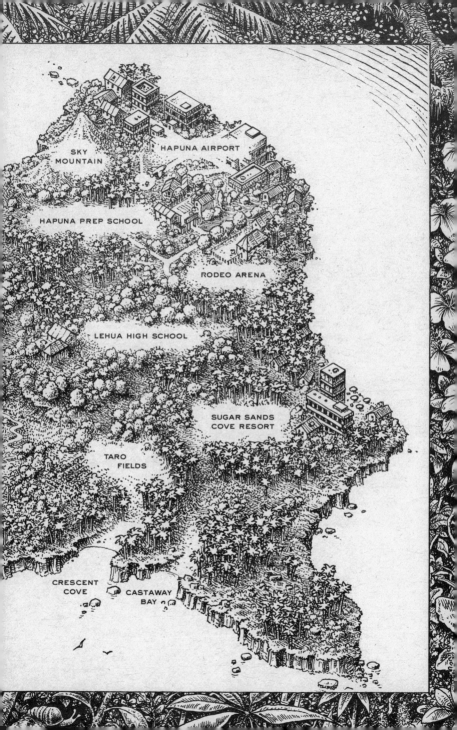

SKY
MOUNTAIN

HAPUNA AIRPORT

HAPUNA PREP SCHOOL

RODEO ARENA

LEHUA HIGH SCHOOL

SUGAR SANDS
COVE RESORT

TARO
FIELDS

CRESCENT
COVE

CASTAWAY
BAY

Chapter One

Mom loves Hawaii.

She's just forgotten.

The words pounded like a memorized poem. Five syllables matched by five more, they'd drummed a rhythm all day long in Darby Carter's mind. They wouldn't stop, even though she was riding her horse.

Excitement over her mother's homecoming had crept into her sleep, too. In last night's dream, Darby's grandfather Jonah had welcomed her mom home by kissing her cheeks, then slipping a flower lei over her black hair to settle around her neck.

Mom will forget her feud with Jonah and move back to Wild Horse Island.

If concentrating could make it so, Darby's wish

would come true.

Ellen Kealoha Carter had sworn never to return to the Hawaiian island where she'd grown up, but she was doing it for Darby, to see her honored—along with her friends Megan and Cade—for finding a shipwrecked colt called Stormbird.

The world stood still as Darby watched gold shimmers of sunshine dance over her horse Hoku's vanilla silk mane. Darby didn't even blink until she realized Hoku had stopped. The filly reached her nose under the round pen's fence and flapped her lips, reaching for a clump of grass.

Darby caught her breath. She'd tumbled so deep into daydreaming, her mind had wandered away from an important fact: The horse she rode—bareback—was barely trained.

On impulse, her hands tugged at the rope rein leading to Hoku's halter.

Bad move. As Hoku backed up in surprise, Darby's body wavered like a candle flame that someone was trying to blow out.

Slow and gentle. Everything had to be that way with a young horse, especially a young mustang used to running free on the Nevada range.

"It's okay, girl," Darby told Hoku, but her horse pawed the dust with a forefoot.

What would Mom think if she saw us right now? Me and my horse . . .

Darby shook off the question. She'd find out

tomorrow, after the presentation at Sugar Sands Cove Resort. Now, at home on 'Iolani Ranch, she'd better focus on riding Hoku.

She let the rein droop, but kept her fingers closed around it. Next, she raised her chin, shrugged her shoulders back, and curved her tailbone toward Hoku's backbone.

The filly shuddered from nose to tail. By the time she understood that Hoku was scaring off a fly, not getting ready to buck, Darby's legs had closed on the sorrel's sides.

Naturally, Hoku broke into a trot that made Darby's teeth clack together and her knees clamp tighter.

Hoku rocked into a lope and Darby's mood lifted, even though she'd hoodwinked herself into believing she was a good rider.

Hoodwinked. Darby imagined riding with her hooded sweatshirt zipped up the back with the hood over her face. She wasn't much of a rider, but she was the only one Hoku had ever known.

If she wanted to keep it that way, it was vital for her mom to decide they should move to Hawaii for good.

She rode with just a halter. For reins, a lead rope was clipped at both ends to the halter ring under Hoku's chin. But tack wasn't important. Darby's body worked with the filly's, sensing the tension and excitement Hoku reflected back to her.

Darby felt the bunched-up muscles in the filly's

hindquarters pushing them around the pen. She leaned forward and rested her hands at the base of the filly's neck. Shoulder blades sculpted by generations of range running slid like polished ivory under her fingers as Hoku's legs pulled at the earth.

I love you, she thought as Hoku carried her past the corral fence. The ranch yard, Sun House, and green hills slipped by. *And I love this ranch,* she thought as tropical breezes sang through her hair.

Saying that her wild horse was under control made about as much sense as a pirate saying he'd commanded the wind to fill his ship's sails, but Darby didn't care. She was happy.

Hoku settled back to a walk. Her head bobbed from side to side, as if checking each dark-hoofed leg.

Dark hooves were supposed to indicate hard feet, less susceptible to injury.

"You're such a good girl."

The filly's elegant ears pricked forward. They'd swivel back if Hoku was listening to her, Darby thought. Then her horse's head swung toward the crunch of tires.

Who was coming down the ranch road? A rooster tail of dust followed the vehicle and a brown cloud surrounded it. It was probably just the ranch manager, Aunty Cathy, bringing her daughter, Megan, home from school.

Although classes were back in session, school had been chaotic since the mini tsunami. That's what the rest of the world was calling it, but to Darby, there'd been nothing small about it.

Now, workers repaired storm damage and talked of dangerous mold growing in the school walls. That could close the school again. So teachers made the most of each classroom moment, shouting over sawing, hammering, and the blasts of nail guns.

Darby could thank Mr. Potter, her friend Ann's dad, for taking her away from all the racket and driving her home from Lehua High School. It was four o'clock and she'd been riding for half an hour instead of dawdling around school.

Actually, she wouldn't have been dawdling. She would have been trying to sneak past the school security officer keeping Lehua High students away from the herd of wild horses penned on the school's football field. Black Lava and his band had been there since the tsunami struck their Crimson Vale valley home, and though Darby and Ann had tried repeatedly, they'd failed to get a good look at the horses. Turned back by school security, Darby knew she would've just ended up doing homework while waiting for Aunty Cathy to pick them up after Megan's soccer practice.

Darby's own practice was important. Tomorrow her mom would arrive on Wild Horse Island. Ellen had never seen her daughter on a horse.

"We've got to be awesome," Darby told Hoku.

Now Darby recognized the faded red fenders, streaked with rust. It wasn't Aunty Cathy and Megan.

It was the farrier's truck.

Hoku's steps slowed. Though the filly was only curious, Darby reined her away from the corral fence.

"No horseshoes for you," Darby assured Hoku.

But then the truck backfired, sounding like a gunshot, and everything happened fast.

Hoku's jump aimed them at the fence rails.

Darby heard the farrier yell, "One-rein stop. Catch her before—"

She knew what he meant, and Darby pulled the left rein toward her knee. She'd done it before, with Navigator, but Hoku didn't react the same way.

Hoku resisted. She pulled back until the rein forced her head to follow. Even then, her body kept charging ahead.

Darby slipped left on Hoku's back and caught a sickening glimpse of the cindery dirt below. If she held tight with her legs, Hoku would lunge forward even though her head was being pulled in the opposite direction.

Darby had to keep her legs loose or risk bringing them both down.

No way I'll let that happen, Darby promised silently.

She released the left rein. As Hoku straightened and looked ahead once more, Darby braced on her filly's withers, then swung her right leg over Hoku's back. Her feet felt frantically for the ground. *Amazing,* Darby thought as she dropped and landed on both boots.

Eyes wide with confusion, nostrils flared to suck in air, Hoku spun around to face Darby.

"You stopped for me," Darby whispered to her horse. Puzzled and a bit scared, Hoku might have kept running. But Darby had left the filly's back unexpectedly, and Hoku was worried about her human.

Darby held out a hand, cupped gently, hoping Hoku would come close and rest her chin there.

The white star marking on Hoku's chest rose with the filly's breaths and she looked away.

I'm asking too much, Darby thought.

"Sorry, girl," Darby said. "That was kinda spooky, wasn't it?"

She eased forward to catch the rein. Then she moved alongside her horse and pressed her cheek against Hoku's hot neck.

Together they sighed. For a few seconds, Darby's eyes almost closed. Through her lashes, she saw nothing but her horse's hair, shot through with gold one minute and fire-red the next.

She wanted to stay like this forever. Breathe in. Breathe out. Feel the sun kneading the kinks out of their backs, hear trade winds rustling in the trees.

"You be careful there, young lady," the farrier called through the open window of his idling truck. "And get Jonah to show you how to 'whoa' before you 'giddyup.'"

Chuckling, the farrier drove on toward the horses that were tethered outside the tack room.

As if he's not to blame for telling me to make a one-rein stop, Darby thought as she glared after him. Still, it was a good thing she hadn't snapped a comeback, because Hoku began shifting with uneasiness again.

Besides, Darby knew she was to blame. She shouldn't have taken the farrier's shouted advice when she knew her horse better than he—or anyone!—did.

Once more, Darby extended her hand toward her filly's nose, but Hoku's head jerked up and she backed away a few steps, rolling her eyes until they showed white.

Darby relaxed her shoulders, letting her body language tell her horse they were safe.

"What happened to you?" an irritated voice called from behind them.

Darby glanced over her shoulder to see her grandfather standing outside the round pen. Jonah's head, black hair graying at his temples, was cocked to one side.

"Nothing," she said, looking back to Hoku.

"So you're trying to stare that filly into doin' what you say?"

"No, I'm just letting her relax. The farrier's truck backfired, she bolted, and I was losing control. . . ."

Great, Darby thought. She'd better stop talking before she confessed any more.

"So you turned her in circles," Jonah finished her sentence.

He started nodding, and Darby guessed he was going to tell her she'd done the right thing.

"No one likes bein' dizzy, 'specially not a horse," Jonah said, then shook his finger at the filly. "That Hoku, she knows she's too big to fall down and get up quick if something's after her."

Darby nodded. "I could feel her trying to keep her balance, but that turning thing? It worked before, when I did it with Navigator."

"He's an experienced horse. He knew goin' around in circles wasn't gettin' him nowhere, so he read your mind and gave you the stop you were after." Jonah shrugged. "You won't see no paniolo trying that merry-go-round stuff."

"What should I have done?" Darby asked.

"Talk to Cade or Kit about bronc stoppin'," Jonah said.

"Bronc stopping? That doesn't sound like something I—"

"Suit yourself," Jonah said. Then his attention shifted to Hoku. "Good the way she waited for you. Shows some respect."

Jonah's compliments were so rare, Darby wanted to whoop in celebration, but her grandfather was already walking away.

"I got to go talk to that horseshoein' thief," Jonah muttered, "and tell him to keep his riding advice to himself."

A bronc stop, Darby repeated silently.

Kit Ely, foreman of 'Iolani Ranch, was a former rodeo rider. She knew that much, but she had no interest in riding like a rodeo cowboy.

And Cade, her grandfather's adopted grandson, might as well be a centaur. He was so much a part of his horse, he probably wouldn't know where to begin teaching her to stop a panicked Hoku. Cade's horse, Joker, never panicked.

Darby led Hoku to the fence.

She had to get back on Hoku and replace the scary backfiring memory with a calm one.

She rode around the corral twice, then managed to open the gate from Hoku's back. She was latching it behind her when light glared in her eyes, making her squint.

Some trick of light made Darby think someone stood on the iron staircase leading up to the apartment over Sun House.

She blinked and no one was there.

She must be sun-dazzled, because she'd really thought someone had motioned her to come up the stairs.

Knock it off, Darby told herself.

Hadn't she just learned a lesson about daydreaming astride a nearly wild horse?

But suddenly Darby thought, *How many times has Aunty Cathy offered to let me go through that stuff of Mom's?*

When Ellen Kealoha had left Wild Horse Island,

swearing she'd never come back, she'd left some possessions behind.

Jonah had stored them in old-fashioned striped hatboxes with ribbon handles, and stowed them in the upstairs apartment he'd built, hoping for his daughter's return.

For years it had stood empty. And even when Aunty Cathy had moved into the apartment with her daughter, Megan, she'd kept the boxes on a desk in the corner.

So what if I looked inside them?

Why shouldn't I —?

Nothing was more important than persuading her mother to stay on Wild Horse Island. To do that, maybe Darby needed to know why Ellen had left in the first place. The striped hatboxes might hold important clues.

Darby smoothed her hand over Hoku's mane, thinking. The filly's ears pricked at the whine of wind through the Zinks' barbed-wire fence.

Darby balanced her mother's privacy against wanting to be prepared. Mom wouldn't have left that stuff behind if it was super secret, would she?

She rode Hoku toward the freshly repaired hitching rack, slid off, looped a rope around her filly's neck, and tied her with a secure knot.

Then she walked quickly toward the apartment stairs.

Aunty Cathy wouldn't mind if she was up there, so why did she feel sneaky?

Darby broke into a jog. There was no time to analyze why.

She bounded up the stairs as fast as she could go, and before she even touched the doorknob, she was picturing how she'd run back downstairs, arms loaded with her mom's stuff, before the white 'Iolani Ranch truck reached home.

 Chapter Two

For the first time in her shaggy little life, Pipsqueak, aka Pip, Megan's white Lhasa Apso dog, didn't bark to announce she was on guard in the Katos' apartment.

So Darby wasn't thinking about anything except the pink-and-white-striped hatboxes until she opened the door and the dog darted out.

"Oh no, you don't." Darby grabbed for Pip, but the dog had already slipped between her ankles. Leaving a whiff of floral doggy shampoo in her wake, Pip headed for the big dogs dozing in the ranch yard.

The little whirlwind of a dog was trouble. Her newest, favorite victim was the orphan piglet Darby had rescued. Pip wasn't headed for the pigpen yet, but her barks had already alerted the Australian shepherds.

Pip incited the big dogs to follow her into all kinds of trouble, from tormenting horses to making Francie, the goat, faint. Because this habit was growing worse instead of better, Jonah had decreed that Pip wasn't allowed outside alone.

"I have more important things to do than be your chaperone," Darby said, but then she saw Pip streaking toward Hoku.

Running in boots wasn't easy, or fast. By the time Darby reached the animals, Hoku was snorting and kicking. The filly hadn't forgotten how Pip had scooted under the fence rails to tease her when she'd been recovering from a barbed-wire injury.

Now, Pip yapped and dodged, bouncing like a piece of popcorn just inches from Hoku's hooves.

Darby's clucking sound stopped Hoku from kicking for only a few seconds, but it was long enough for Darby to scoop up Pip.

Turning back toward Sun House, Darby lectured the dog. "It's a wonder Jonah allows you to live here. Every animal on this place has a purpose, and I sure don't know what yours—ouch!" Pip's nails scratched Darby's arm as the dog squirmed. "Forget it. You'd better watch out for Hoku. She could really hurt you. Even though you're a pest, I don't want that to happen."

She carried Pip upstairs and inside, released her, and wondered why the dog was growling and wagging her tail at the same time.

"This must be fun for you," Darby grumbled.

She'd just grabbed the two pink-and-white-striped hatboxes when she heard tires bumping over the cattle guard at the 'Iolani Ranch entrance. A glance out the upstairs window told her the farrier was leaving, but Megan and Aunty Cathy sat in the idling ranch truck, waiting to drive in when the farrier had passed.

And here she was in their house.

Heat flooded Darby's face. She was allowed to be here. She had permission to look at her mother's stuff. So why did she feel like a burglar?

"Stay," she ordered Pip.

As Darby clomped downstairs, Aunty Cathy and Megan climbed out of the parked truck. Then they stared up at her.

Aunty Cathy pushed her brown-blond hair behind one ear and considered the hatboxes.

Megan's high color was more than her usual post-soccer practice flush as she said, "Cool, you decided to look at that stuff!"

"Yeah," Darby said. She couldn't blame her friend for her excitement. Megan had lived with boxes of secrets in the corner of her home for over a year. Who wouldn't be curious?

"Now that my mom's coming for sure, I just want to see if, you know, there's more to why she left." Darby took a deep breath, then blurted out the rest of it. "I want to find something that will help me make her want to stay."

Aunty Cathy started to say something, hesitated, then closed her mouth.

"Don't you think I should do it?" Darby asked.

"That's a tough one," Aunty Cathy said. "You know for sure that she's coming?"

Darby nodded. "Aunt Babe was right. She told me to tell Mom that it would be a special favor to her if Mom came in time for the presentation. You know, so that the TV cameras show Ellen Kealoha at Sugar Sands Cove Resort."

"Playground of the stars," Megan said, laughing.

"If she's going to be here tomorrow, you could ask her permission," Aunty Cathy said.

Darby's stomach sank. Was it disappointment or embarrassment?

"I won't tell you not to do it, but if you're asking me for advice . . ." Aunty Cathy's voice trailed off.

"I am," Darby admitted, even though Megan rolled her eyes.

"Just let your feelings be your guide," Aunty Cathy suggested. "If you come across something that feels too personal, set it aside."

"But Jonah's the one who packed it up," Megan interrupted. "There can't be anything that private, can there?"

Aunty Cathy didn't have to say a word. The look she shot her daughter was enough.

"Sorry," Megan apologized. "This is none of my business." She pretended to zip her lips, then slung her soccer bag over her shoulder before heading up the stairs.

"Jonah *did* pack it all up, and he planned to send it to Ellen when she got settled on the mainland," Aunty Cathy said. "But she didn't send him an address until years later."

Darby couldn't imagine doing that to her parents.

"Are you sure?" Darby asked.

Aunty Cathy put a hand on Darby's shoulder. "No, honey, I'm not. Jonah hasn't been very"—she searched for the right word—"forthcoming? Or open, about your mother."

Jonah wasn't open about much of anything, Darby thought, but she said, "I just hope they can work things out."

"At least they'll be on the same side of the Pacific Ocean," Aunty Cathy said. "That's a start."

Darby stashed the boxes in her bedroom, then rushed outside. Mist was creeping in, blotting out edges of hills, and though it was still warm, Darby knew she'd feel soggy before she finished caring for Francie, the goat, and her orphan piglet, Pigolo.

She glanced at Hoku, still tied by her neck rope at the hitching rail. Even though the filly nickered and pawed for attention, she'd save Hoku for last.

"You're feeding early," Jonah observed as she emerged from Pigolo's pen.

"Homework," Darby said, which was the truth,

even though she usually left her weekend homework for Sunday night.

"Hmm," Jonah grunted.

Darby didn't stay to talk. If she did, her grandfather was sure to make a crack about fattening the piglet for Fourth of July dinner.

Instead, she jogged to untie Hoku. Unclipping one end of the tangerine-and-white-striped rope, Darby led the filly toward her corral.

At least, she tried to.

"*Ku'uipo,*" she crooned when the horse braced all four legs and refused to move. "That means 'sweetheart,' remember? If you're going to be a Hawaiian horse, you might as well learn the language."

Ears pointed toward the end of the dirt road that ran past the old fox cages and her own corral, Hoku ignored Darby.

Darby brushed the beads of moisture from her eyelashes and followed the filly's stare, but she didn't spot anything worth Hoku's attention.

"What do you see, girl?" Darby asked.

Mist obscured the place where the road came to an end and the rolling hills began. She could picture the grassland ahead. If you went that way long enough, you'd come to a place called the fold, where 'Iolani Ranch crested and fell like a wave of green velvet.

Darby's pulse pounded as she remembered Black Lava lurking among the hills. Hoku had confronted the wild stallion there. Was she remembering, too?

But Black Lava was corralled with his herd now at Lehua High School, and Hoku looked curious, not bold and ready to chase off an intruder.

"Ow!"

The lead rope jerked tight around Darby's hand. Bones grated against each other.

Amputation, Darby thought, but the lead rope slipped free of her hand as Hoku bolted.

Darby cradled the hand against her ribs, but only for a second. Everyone on the ranch had warned her about wrapping the lead rope around her hand.

Her hand ached with every stride she took after Hoku. Her filly wasn't moving too fast. Her gait was a cautious trot. Still, the pain could have been avoided, Darby lectured herself. She'd never be so stupid again.

She moved up along her filly's right side, determined to snag the trailing rope with the hand that didn't hurt. But then Hoku skidded to a stop.

Playful as a colt, the sorrel tossed her nose in the direction of something only she could see, and gave a half buck.

An invitation to kick up your heels, Darby thought as her eyes investigated each dip, curve, and shadow in the grass, hunting for the creature Hoku was greeting. *Whoever you are, please don't accept!*

There. A black-and-white form emerged from the mist and resolved itself into a beautiful paint horse.

Don't I know you? Darby asked silently.

The strange horse gave a nicker and kept her eyes on Darby. The paint approached quietly. If Hoku went cavorting off, catching her would take all night.

Since the horses were still assessing each other, Darby raised her left arm in tiny increments toward the lead rope.

The last time she'd seen the horse, she'd been brindled by shadows, not blurred with dusk. Medusa, Black Lava's lead mare, had been disciplining the pinto, keeping her in the herd with a savage bite just above the tail.

And then the volcano erupted, Darby thought. *No wonder it took me a minute to remember.*

She couldn't see the mare well enough to spot the bite. Besides, it had been weeks ago.

The paint whisked her tail from side to side. Head lowered in friendliness, she strolled toward Hoku.

Darby refused to let herself be hypnotized by the beautiful horse, but the closer she got, the more the mare smelled of a combination of grass and violets.

Do it now, Darby ordered herself.

Pretending she wasn't recapturing Hoku, Darby raised her left arm the last inches she needed to grasp the lead rope.

Hoku didn't mind, but the black-and-white horse stopped with one hoof still raised.

Friendly, but cautious.

Tame, but wild.

"Where'd you come from?" Darby whispered.

The paint reversed in midstep. She backed away, slowly at first, then whirled in the other direction and disappeared.

Hoku neighed after the horse.

"Shh," Darby hushed her filly, then scolded her. "Jonah's pretty much had his fill of wild horses, so let's just work on you being the best of your breed, okay?"

Hoku blew a silvery blast of breath through her nostrils, and accompanied Darby back to the corral. She allowed herself to be slipped into her corral, and stood waiting for a few forkfuls of hay.

"Good girl," Darby whispered to her horse. "I'll see you in the morning."

But when Darby glanced over her shoulder toward the fold and caught Hoku doing the same, she knew both of them were pretending they weren't sorry to see the mysterious horse go.

Secrets were not Darby's favorite thing. She wanted to burst into Sun House and ask Jonah, Cathy, and Megan about the black-and-white trespasser. But that might lead to a wild horse hunt, or a flurry of phone calls to neighbors, and someone else showing up for dinner. Since she already had those hidden hatboxes in her room and she was eager to discover *their* secrets, Darby sat on the entrance hall bench, tugged off her boots, and headed for the door at the end of the hall.

Her snug room still smelled faintly of fresh paint.

The mist outside didn't blot out a sunbeam that slanted in her window, turning the leaves of her lucky bamboo plant spring green before falling onto a polished wood floor the color of peanut butter.

For a minute, Darby couldn't remember what her room at home in Pacific Pinnacles looked like. She could only picture that beautiful, mysterious mare.

Horses were herd animals, she lectured herself. Why wouldn't a lone mare be drawn to other horses? After all, Hoku was too. There was no mystery in that.

She peeked under her bed. The boxes were still there.

Pulling them out, Darby decided to open the boxes while sitting on the bed, instead of at her desk.

Before she plopped on the bed, she closed her bedroom door. Hands on hips, she regarded it. The door didn't have a lock.

What if she wedged the back of her desk chair under the doorknob, so that no one could get in?

"Stop it," she whispered to herself. "If you feel so guilty, is this something you should be doing?"

She looked away from the door and studied the two round boxes.

What was the worst thing that could happen if she looked inside them? This was modern-day America, not ancient Greece, or wherever the mythical Pandora's box was opened to let pain and evil into the world.

Megan had made the point that Jonah had packed Ellen's things away, so it wasn't like Darby would be the first to see them. Besides, if she could learn what had driven a wedge between her mother and grandfather, maybe she could try to mend it.

That's the important thing, Darby decided, and she sat down on her bed.

Leaning back against her headboard, Darby opened the first box.

Clippings from Lehua High School's newspaper lay on top. Her mom had gone there, too. All but one of them were about people and events that meant nothing to Darby.

"*Diary of Anne Frank* a Sad Success," read the headline on a review of the school play from years ago. Not only had Ellen played the lead role, but the reviewer said she'd made Anne come alive in a way that had playgoers departing in tears after the final curtain.

"Good going, Mom," Darby whispered, but her smile became a wince when she flattened out three letters that were folded one inside the other, and read them.

They were rejection letters from colleges.

"Because the admissions process is such a competitive one . . ."

"We were honored by your application to . . ."

"Few high school seniors have your qualifications, however . . ."

All three letters said pretty much the same thing.

Though Ellen Kealoha had high grades and outstanding test scores, each college sought more well-rounded students. If Ellen planned to major in drama, she needed more stage or even backstage experience.

Poor Mom, Darby thought.

Next, she studied a professionally printed photograph of Jonah and Ellen with Prettypaint, the horse that Tutu rode now.

Tutu was Darby's great-grandmother. A warm and gentle woman, Tutu lived in a rain-forest cottage with Prettypaint and an owl who was friendly only to her. Known as an herbal healer and wise woman, Tutu accepted Darby's intuition for understanding horses as significant but not strange. She and Jonah shared the trait, and for all Darby knew, her mother had once been the same.

Prettypaint was young in the picture. Maybe a yearling. The photo looked like it had been taken at a horse show.

Pale gray with bluish spots on her heels, Prettypaint wore a red ribbon on her halter. Jonah and her mom looked proud as each held one side of the filly's halter, but they both also had an arm crossed across their stomachs and hands fisted with tension.

Was she imagining things, or was she really seeing clues leading up to Mom's decision to run away from the island?

Jonah hadn't packed things in any kind of order, that was for sure. A rosebud corsage and a triangular note folded origami tight and decorated with smeared pencil-drawn hearts was crammed in with an official-looking letter that wasn't even Mom's.

The letter, from the American Quarter Horse Association (AQHA), notified Jonah that Ellen Kealoha's college scholarship would be awarded to another deserving student if she didn't claim it in six weeks.

Darby hadn't known that the AQHA gave scholarships. That was something to remember. But why hadn't her mom snapped it up?

Darby's curiosity intensified when she found the stack of report cards tied with a ribbon like love letters.

Wow, of course she knew her mom was smart, but since elementary school, Ellen had earned almost straight A's.

Darby leafed through a bunch of honor certificates, including an award from Lehua High's foreign language department and another for perfect attendance.

Then came Mom's senior-year report card. Her grades had all changed to C's.

The next box was heavier because it held three yearbooks.

Darby flipped through them, looking alphabetically until she found her mother.

This is like time travel, she thought, arranging the yearbooks side by side. Mom was beautiful in every picture, but the sparkle in her ponytailed freshman photograph was gone by her sophomore year. Her smile looked forced and her teeth didn't show. By junior year, she looked, well, kind of stuck-up.

Darby gazed into the mirror on the other side of her room and imitated her mother's pose. She lifted her chin, tipped her head, and raised an eyebrow, but the effect wasn't the same, because Mom had really loaded on the black eyeliner and crimson lipstick.

No yearbook for senior year. Had the money for the keepsake gone to buy hay instead or had her mom taken it with her when she left?

Darby was still searching for another yearbook when her fingers grazed the black leather diary.

It slipped free from the stuff around it as if it had been waiting for her.

Holding the book in both hands, Darby argued with herself.

Nothing is more private than a diary.

But Mom left it behind.

Not for *you*!

How secret is a diary when it's not even locked?

She didn't know she was going to have a daughter when she wrote it.

Yeah, there's got to be some juicy stuff in there.

How would you feel if *she* read *your* diary?

If it meant living happily ever after on Wild Horse Island, I'd forgive her.

Haven't you ever heard that curiosity killed the cat?

With stiff, good-girl fingers, Darby was returning the diary to the hatbox when the latch flopped open. A clump of pages, loosened from years of opening and closing, fell out and plopped on the bedspread, right in front of her.

It's a sign, Darby decided.

"Dinner!" Aunty Cathy's shout from the kitchen startled Darby.

She latched the diary without replacing the fallen pages.

"Coming!" she yelled back.

Carefully, she returned the diary to its place among the yearbooks. Then she stood up and wedged both hatboxes back under her bed.

With a cautious glance at her closed bedroom door, Darby folded back her white tufted bedspread and slipped the clump of pages under her pillow.

"I'll decide later," she whispered to herself.

Then she smoothed the bedspread back in place and left.

Chapter Three

It figured that on a night when she was preoccupied with a mystery mare, her mom's arrival, the pages under her pillow, and Hoku's spooky reaction to the one-rein stop, there'd be five people at the dinner table.

In celebration of tomorrow's ceremony, Aunty Cathy had invited Cade to dinner.

As Darby came down the hall from her bedroom, Cade crossed the threshold of Sun House. Turning his hat in his hands and shifting from foot to foot, he glanced at her and nodded but kept talking to Jonah.

As she passed, Darby heard Cade confide his uneasiness at intruding on a family dinner. Still, he'd accepted the invitation. That was a first since Darby had been here.

"Better than sitting alone while Kit meets his girl-friend and new horse in town, yeah?" Jonah asked him.

"Yeah," Cade agreed.

Given the chance, Darby would have chosen time inside the Animal Rescue Society barn, watching Kit and his girlfriend, Cricket, bond with Kit's newly adopted mustang, Medusa. On the other hand, maybe Cade hadn't been invited.

The table was set on the lanai, one of Darby's favorite spots on the ranch. The wide balcony over-looked hundreds of green acres of ranchland, grazed by horses and cattle of many colors.

An evening rainbow arched among the hills. Darby had just wished on it when Aunty Cathy said, "I seem to remember negotiating a deal to share dinner-cooking responsibilities. Not with you, Cade, but with these other three."

"Mom, you won't help your own cause by making dinners like this." Megan held up a pinkish forkful. "I mean, if you make guava shrimp curry and I slap together Spam sandwiches, who's going to show up on my nights?"

Darby nodded. She could follow directions to make a basic casserole, but the simplest thing on this table was rice. Even using a rice cooker, she couldn't strike a balance between burning it brown and leaving it pale and soupy.

"Thanks for inviting me *tonight*," Cade said.

Jonah gave an amused snort and Megan stuck out her tongue at Cade.

Darby tried to figure out what was different about Cade as, with the faintest of smiles, he helped himself to more macaroni salad.

As usual, Cade wore a roomy paniolo shirt of beige linen. It looked just like his others. Brown skin, brown eyes, blond hair in a tight paniolo braid—all that was the same. Darby couldn't have explained what it was, but since he'd stood up to Manny, his abusive step-father, there'd been a change in Cade.

He quit chewing and met her stare. Darby looked down at her plate.

"I'll cook tomorrow," she volunteered.

"Your mother will be here, and I want you to have time to talk with her," Aunty Cathy said.

"How long is she staying?" Megan asked.

If Darby hadn't been trying to look anyplace except at Cade, she might not have noticed Jonah's fingers tightening on his fork.

Please let them get along, Darby thought, but she didn't say it.

"Just the weekend, I think," Darby said. "She mentioned she had to shoot an important scene on Wednesday."

"I can't help it," Megan said. "I'm excited to meet a real star."

"I'm glad she'll be here for the ceremony at Babe's," Aunty Cathy said.

"What will we do with all that lovely money?" Megan stared off the lanai as if bags of gold floated near the pasture rainbow.

"I know what I'll do," Cade said.

"Yeah?" Jonah asked.

Cade nodded, flushed, and said, "I'm saving for land of my own."

Jonah frowned, then cleared his throat.

"You know, as my hanai'd son, that . . ." His voice was constricted, as if something had wrapped around his neck.

Aunty Cathy leaned forward, forearms bracketing her plate, as if she could help.

". . . you're welcome here, forever."

"Yeah," Cade said.

"Would it be rude to ask if the Crimson Vale place belongs to your mom or Manny?" Darby asked.

"Sure it would," Cade said, "but since I don't know the answer, I guess that's okay."

It was then, as he tried not to laugh at her, that Darby realized it was Cade's face that looked different.

"Did you shave?" she asked.

"Oh my gosh!" Megan put a hand over her eyes as if she was too embarrassed to look at Darby.

"What?" Darby yelped. Why would he be self-conscious about shaving?

"Are you six years old?" Megan asked.

"Mekana," Jonah reprimanded softly.

"Sorry," Megan apologized. "It's just the very first time, I think, and that means our Cade is all grown-up." When her sugary tone evoked no response from Cade, Megan moved to playfully sock his shoulder but Cade blocked the punch and gave a long-suffering sigh.

"Time for the news," Jonah said, pushing back from the table. "C'mon, Cade, watch TV with me while the *wahines* clean up."

"That means 'the women,' right?" Darby asked.

Aunty Cathy stood and began gathering plates from the table like a seasoned waitress. "Don't let him get a rise out of you."

"Why not?" Megan pretended to glare after Jonah as he turned on the television and settled into his favorite chair.

"I have pineapple whipped cream cake in the kitchen," Aunty Cathy said.

"Maybe we won't share," Darby teased.

"I heard that," Jonah called after them.

Stuffed full of dessert, Darby was leaning back in her chair on the lanai, mulling over what she should do about her mother's diary, when Megan interrupted her thoughts.

"Unfair!" Megan shouted.

"What is?" Darby asked.

She stared at the girl she sometimes called "sis" and reconsidered the connection. Megan's shout was so random, Darby had no idea what Megan was talking about.

"Didn't you hear what he said?"

"He" who? Darby thought.

Aunty Cathy gestured toward the living room as Megan went on, "He's saying something about two of the three young people being honored tomorrow helped save Moku Lio Hihiu's wild horses during the flood. He left me out, even though I was over on Oahu representing my school."

". . . dramatic new rescue footage you'll see only on Channel Two . . ." As the voice of Channel Two reporter Mark Larson floated to the lanai from the television in the living room, Darby understood.

"I've got to watch," Darby said, and followed after Aunty Cathy and Megan as they left the lanai.

Megan sprawled on the floor in front of the television. Aunty Cathy sat on the couch without crowding Cade.

Not that he would have noticed, Darby thought. Sitting there with his gaze fixed on the television screen, hands resting on his knees, Cade looked hypnotized.

Darby stopped behind Jonah's big chair. After one glimpse of the news report, she didn't want to go closer.

She'd forgotten how awful the island had looked just after the tsunami. Shooting from the TV helicopter, the camera showed tobacco-brown water strewn with debris and dead animals.

When reporter Mark Larson, wearing his trademark Hawaiian shirt, filled the screen, Darby let out the breath she'd been holding.

"By morning, the *kai a Pele*, Pele's tide—traditionally a punishment from her sister the sea goddess, angry because Pele poured lava into her realm—had receded." The reporter spoke in a storyteller's voice as the camera scanned the dawn sky, then dropped to show the wet, huddled horses.

"The wild herd had been stranded for twenty-four hours. Although the tsunami took some of them, the horses on the spit of lava rock were also prey to rain, sharks, and floating debris. Surrounded by danger, the horses were not about to come ashore on their own. Finally, they were rescued by dedicated equestrian volunteers."

"Hoku!"

"Don't tip me over, Granddaughter," Jonah said when Darby bumped the back of his recliner at the sight of her horse on television.

It was weird to see Cade, Kit, and herself riding three across. Reflections of Joker, Navigator, and Hoku showed on the wet sand.

It was like a movie, except that she recalled images the camera didn't show, like Kit tying down his Stetson with a stampede strap and Cade leaving behind his prized hala hat and green poncho, going barefoot in jeans and a white T-shirt into the wind and waves.

The camera pulled back to show an earthquake-damaged house, a flooded taro field, plastic fence set up to funnel the horses to safety, and finally the red trucks with firefighters beside them, waiting.

And then things really got weird. The view shifted to Mark Larson inside a helicopter. He shouted over the rotors as he pointed toward a trail of white spume on the water below.

"And here comes another volunteer, there on the Jet Ski." His voice deepened and took a reprimanding tone. "A misguided soul, to judge by our interview with the Animal Rescue's expert. She indicated that the mechanical rescue of wild animals—wait, can you get that?" Mark Larson stopped his commentary to talk to the camera operator.

Suddenly there was a shot of Manny steering at high speed toward Hoku.

"Viewers, I have an unconfirmed report that the man on the Jet Ski is Manuel Billfish and the girl on horseback is Darby Kealoha, Lehua High School student and great-niece to 'Babe' Kealoha Borden.

"Mr. Billfish was ordered not to take a mechanized vehicle into the water during the rescue attempt. Harassment of a federally protected species, like the wild horse, is a felony."

For a moment the sound grew too scratchy to understand, and even though she knew how this story ended, the sight of her frightened horse made Darby's fingernails sink into the fabric of Jonah's chair.

Seeing the events again, Darby remembered

hating Manny. Her brave horse had tolerated strange weather, sounds, and smells, and then Manny had zoomed at her with a snarling metal beast.

Darby didn't remember Hoku rearing. She didn't remember falling.

"Hold a good thought for that young lady under the storm waters," Mark Larson said on-screen, "and we'll move in closer to help if we can."

Megan took an audible breath and said, "You sure stayed under for a long time."

Aunty Cathy's gasp was almost a scream, as she pointed. A close-up showed a piece of corrugated iron rocking on Jet Ski–generated waves. It bounced about a foot into the air.

"That was you. I saw your hands, your head," Aunty Cathy said. "That's what bruised your head, that big piece of metal."

"I don't think so," Darby faltered, but she touched her head, trying to remember.

For a split second, the camera showed Joker leaping waves. Cade hurled himself off the Appaloosa. Hair streaming loose, he hit the water.

"A woman is coming to Darby Kealoha's rescue," Mark Larson said, but the mutter that followed made it clear he'd realized his mistake.

The jiggling camera caught Cade's ripped T-shirt before the focus widened to take in his hands. He gripped Hoku's rein while he kept Darby's head above the waves.

"I beg your pardon, viewers. . . ."

If Mark Larson said anything interesting after that, no one heard. Everything was drowned out by Megan's laughter. She'd clearly gotten a kick out of Cade being called a woman, but Darby was preoccupied with a slow-motion replay on the television.

"Crazy superhero, yeah?" Jonah said. He leaned toward the couch from his chair and gave Cade's shoulder a shake.

"Naw," Cade said. He looked at the floor as the TV reporter's voice continued.

Darby watched herself act like a . . . what? She could only come up with an expression she'd read. She'd acted like an *ungrateful wretch*. Had she been so dizzy and bewildered, hypothermic, maybe, out there in the ocean, that she'd really shoved Cade away hard enough that he'd made a big white splash, so she could climb onto Hoku without help?

"I don't remember it like that," Darby said, not really talking to anyone until she turned toward Cade and said, "Thank you."

Megan was still laughing her head off, so probably no one heard.

Except Cade.

"He mea iki," he said, which she took for *You're welcome.* Then, as the TV report ended, Cade grumbled, "I hope they never show that again."

"Me too," Darby said, but her mom had told her about news services picking up local stories and printing them in newspapers all over the world. TV news services must be the same.

That meant people all over Hawaii, maybe all over the world, would see Manny's intentional harassment of Hoku. That was good. He'd stay in jail.

They'd also see her fall. Oddly, that didn't embarrass her. What mattered was that Hoku, a mustang born free and wild, had stood by her human, just like she had today.

Yes! Excited chills raced down Darby's arms. This was a dramatic story. Some news service might broadcast the story in Nevada. She could picture her friend Samantha Forster dancing in delight over the wonder of wild horses.

Darby's smile faded as she realized worldwide viewers would see Cade ride to her rescue. She grimaced. That part, she could do without.

"Megan, it's not that funny," Aunty Cathy said, finally.

Wiping tears of laughter from her eyes, Megan said, "Oh, Mom, it is, too. They thought Cade was a girl." Another round of giggles shook her, but she held up a finger because she had more to say. "But the good thing is, Cade will have a chance to set the record straight tomorrow."

"No," Cade began.

"See if you kept that torn shirt, yeah?" Jonah teased.

The whole situation was a happy one, Darby told

herself. Pouting because she looked like she'd nearly drowned instead of swimming like a champion was childish. She decided to leave the room before she ruined everyone's fun.

"I'm going to go do the dishes," Darby said, wheeling toward the kitchen.

"I'll help," Cade added.

"Me too." Megan's voice overlapped Cade's and he shrugged.

"Then I'll go hide in the bunkhouse. Hope Kit was too busy with Medusa to see that." He pointed at the television, almost smiling.

Darby stood in the kitchen doorway, about to describe the black-and-white mare to Cade, as he sat on the entrance hall bench to tug on his boots.

"Okay?" Cade said under his breath without looking up.

Darby wasn't sure what Cade meant. Was it okay he'd rescued her? She didn't like being a damsel in distress any more than she liked being the *wahine* cleaning the kitchen, but Cade was standing taller than he had since she'd first met him.

Confronting Manny, and now this . . .

Still seated, Cade jerked down the cuffs of his jeans and raised his eyes to her. His jaw was set hard. "I know you woulda pulled yourself out."

Darby noticed Megan walking toward the kitchen, still looking amused.

"Yeah, after I swallowed a couple gallons of salt

water," Darby said, then added, "Thanks for having my back, Cade, really."

Cade stood, shrugged, and pulled his hat over his eyes, but not far enough to hide his flush. Then he shouldered past the front door and into the night before Darby had a chance to say anything about the mysterious mare.

Chapter Four

"My father treats me like a slave!"

The words in Ellen Kealoha's high school diary were written in red ink that bled through the page. After reading that first sentence on the pages that had fallen out of the black leather book, Darby couldn't stop.

"He says I don't understand, but he won't explain!!! When I beg him to, he walks away. Always. He can't think of a good enough argument because *I'm right* when I tell him he's too stingy to hire a ranch hand when he's got a kid he can work half to death!!!

"Too bad if she's a REALLY TALENTED ACTRESS. I wouldn't even care about the work if he'd let me ACT. Mr. Taylor says I'm good and his new student teacher Mrs. Martindale said so, too."

Darby looked up from the page for a second. Mrs. Martindale? Could it be the same Mrs. Martindale who was her Creative Writing teacher this year?

"He couldn't come see me in the play because he had to stay home with Mom. Obviously, I get that, but I showed him my *Anne Frank* review and he was proud! He said to go ahead and try out again and he'd come see me. But what's the use of auditioning for a play if he won't let me stay after school for rehearsal? He makes me come *home* right away, every single day!"

Darby thought of Mrs. Martindale again. Even though her Creative Writing teacher had wrongfully accused her of plagiarism, she'd later apologized. But that wasn't what Darby was remembering.

When Mrs. Martindale had suggested Darby be on the staff of the school's literary magazine, Jonah had asked if that met after school.

Mrs. Martindale had said yes, but added that the school was getting a new after-school activity bus for kids from outlying areas—like Darby.

And when Jonah made excuses, Mrs. Martindale had winked at Darby and insisted they'd work something out.

It was strange, Darby thought, that Jonah, who let her go on all kinds of adventures all over the island, had acted like she had to come straight home from school and do chores. Almost like it had been a reflex, left over from her mom's high school days.

Was that possible?

Darby started to turn the page, but it was stuck to the next one. Carefully, she worked her fingertip around the edge. When the pages parted, she found pink flower petals, a scrap of newsprint, and just two sentences written on the page.

"I like being with the horses, I love Prettypaint and Ebony and all of them, but the real me is on that stage. Can't I have both?"

Darby was smiling until she managed to read the small newspaper print on the short article.

"*Alexandra Rojas Kealoha* died at her home on 'Iolani Ranch following a long illness. Wife of Jonah Kealoha, mother of Ellen Kealoha, daughter of famed soccer player Roberto 'Boot' Rojas and schoolteacher Ikena Kamakau Rojas, she was born on Moku Lio Hihiu. . . ."

Darby's gaze raced over the words three times before she realized she was reading her grandmother's obituary. Her mom's mother had died while Ellen had been a freshman in high school.

"One year older than me," Darby whispered into her bedroom's stillness. She closed her eyes against the burn of tears. Though she'd never known her grandmother, Darby couldn't help putting herself in her mom's place.

Once the pang of empathy faded, Darby looked at the obituary again. She studied her bloodlines like she would those of a horse. Then she got out her own diary, copied names, and drew a diagram of her heritage. It didn't go back far, but it was cool that there were Hawaiian names in every generation. Rojas was Hispanic, but from which country? And Carter, her dad's family, what kind of name was that? It would be fun to find out.

All of a sudden Darby sat up straighter. Since her mother had said she had enough money to pay for her own Tahiti-to-Hawaii plane ticket, Darby hadn't used her reward money. Maybe she could buy her dad a ticket to Hawaii!

When Jonah knocked on her bedroom door, Darby jumped and looked around quickly. The hatboxes were under her bed. All she had to do was flop her bedspread over five pages that were the size of her hand. So she did.

"Come in," she called.

Jonah the horse charmer took one look at her face and said, "What are you up to?"

Darby shrugged her shoulders so high they almost grazed her earlobes.

"Not schoolwork," he said, but his eyes fixed on her notebooks.

"I'm writing in my diary," she admitted.

Jonah nodded and his face took on such a faraway expression, Darby expected him to say, *Your mother had a diary*, but he didn't.

"I'm all ready for tomorrow," Darby said.

"What's to get ready?" Jonah asked.

Darby gestured at the wrinkle-free blouse and new jeans hanging on her closet door.

"My mom always says you can't go wrong with a white blouse and nice jewelry," Darby said.

"Oh, she does? Which jewelry are you wearing?"

"Okay, so I've only got the white blouse," Darby said, "but I thought she'd be so glad to see me, she'd let that pass."

Jonah stared at the window above her bed. When he spoke again, he pretty much confirmed he hadn't been listening to her. "We'll drive over, let people see you get a reward for your work tracking down Stormbird—that's what Babe calls the colt you found, yeah?—and come home."

"And meet my mom there," Darby said pointedly.

Ellen's plane from Tahiti had to stop on Oahu before it hopped over to Moku Lio Hihiu, but she should arrive with plenty of time to drive to Aunt Babe's resort.

Jonah knew all that, but he changed the subject, tilting his head in the direction of the living room.

"Pretty exciting stuff on the news, yeah?"

"Pretty exciting," she echoed.

"That Hoku, she stayed right by you."

"I know!" Darby didn't mean to wrap her arms around herself in delight. It just happened.

"It's that Quarter Horse blood showin' through," Jonah teased.

"I'm pretty sure it's mustang loyalty to her herd.

Me," she told him.

"You get some sleep. Big day tomorrow," Jonah said.

"Good night," Darby called as her grandfather closed the door.

She jumped up, brushed her teeth, put on her nightgown, and crawled into bed. But she wasn't done for the night.

She had to read the rest of her mom's diary, because talking to Jonah had made her realize that as Ellen had grown into her teens, the one thing that kept her and Jonah together was horses.

What if I could make that happen again? Darby asked herself. She thought she could, but first she had to figure out why Jonah had started keeping her mom home to do chores instead of letting her act.

Darby kept reading, and though she didn't find the answer, she discovered what her mom had done about it. To get back at Jonah, Ellen had quit riding.

This is too depressing, Darby thought. She was about to tuck the pages back in the diary when she saw, "A wild stallion, a flash of silver and black under the candlenut tree, came to visit tonight. He was amazing—a horse made of starlight and black satin."

Darby repeated the words to herself. They sang through her like a magical spell.

Then she sucked in a breath, got up on her knees, and looked out her bedroom window. She couldn't see much through the glass reflection of her own face, but there was the candlenut tree, and right there she'd seen the Shining Stallion, which was probably Black Lava, coming to steal mares for his herd.

She shivered. This was her mom's old bedroom. Why hadn't anyone told her?

But that didn't matter half as much as what happened next in the diary.

"He came for Ebony," Ellen had written in tiny letters. "A wild black-and-white paint stallion."

It could be a coincidence, but what if it wasn't? What if the mare she'd just seen was descended from this creature of starlight and black satin?

Keep reading.

". . . I let down the rails on Ebony's pen. In the morning, I'll run down before anyone else is awake and put them back up. I'm setting my alarm now. I know Ebony won't run away, but if she has a foal by . . ."

That was the end, the last line on the last page Darby had allowed herself to read. She read it over three times before she looked up in amazement.

Never, not in a million years, would she have guessed her mother could be such a bad kid. *Could Mom's trick have created the mystery mare that I saw today?*

Darby bounced on her bed in frustration. She wanted to read more, but a deal was a deal, even if it was with your conscience.

She turned off her bedside lamp before slipping out of bed and reaching underneath for the hatbox.

She lifted the lid—careful not to feel around for the diary's smooth cover, since that would be too tempting—and dropped the pages in.

Moonlight streamed through Darby's window. She still wasn't sleepy, so she retrieved a book. They'd read a short story by Madeleine L'Engle in their literature textbook, and she'd liked it so much, she'd gone to the school library and checked out a novel by the writer.

Curling on her side, Darby read.

She was smiling as the book dropped from her hands, and the link she'd found to her mother, through her diary, comforted her. Her mom was coming. Tomorrow.

Probably today, but she didn't open her eyes to check the clock, and as Darby drifted to sleep, images of the black leather diary reshaped themselves into an aristocratic mare named Ebony, then shrank to a dancing foal, daughter of a black-and-silver stallion.

It was four o'clock in the morning when Kimo's truck rattled into the ranch yard. Then Darby heard Hoku's neigh. She knew that sound by heart.

"What's wrong?" Darby slid off her bed and hit the floor, but she was up, walking and talking before her eyes opened.

She managed to open her bedroom door, but collided with Jonah in the dark hallway.

Her grandfather turned her around by her shoulders.

"Go back to bed," he told her. Chuckling, he walked behind her, steering her toward her warm blankets. "A few steers'll be keepin' an appointment at Hapuna harbor. The guys plan to get an early start before the roads are clogged with people coming to see you get your big money."

Darby heard a clang. Jonah must have bumped into the clothes hanger on her closet door holding her white blouse. She hoped it didn't fall and get wrinkled, but she concentrated on finding that comfy spot on her pillow. Still, he'd said something about steers and money, and Hoku had called out a question, hadn't she?

"Huh?" Darby asked. "*What's* happening?"

"Kimo and Kit want to get back in time to come for Babe's media luau. . . ."

Darby's eyes opened for a second. She was pretty sure that wouldn't make sense, even if she was wide awake.

"And me, I'm up figurin' how I can make enough from each shipment of cattle to pay Kimo and Kit half of what they're worth. . . ."

She understood that, but she didn't want to think about it. Not now.

Megan bounced on Darby's bed three hours later. "I can't believe the phone didn't wake you up. It's rung like a million times!"

"I was up late," Darby explained. She pulled herself to

a sitting position and rubbed her cheek, pretty sure she'd used the hardback book for a pillow. "The phone?"

"I think everyone we know from school's called to make sure our award ceremony is at eleven."

"Really? Like who?" Darby asked through a yawn.

"Like everyone. Ann's called twice, a bunch of people from the soccer team and the swim team, and most of the neighbors."

"Okay," Darby said, but then her heart did a double jump. Her mom could already be at the airport in Tahiti.

"Want to know what I think?" Megan asked.

"Sure."

"Half of them want to be our friends because we're about to be rich, and the other half want a look at your mom, the celebrity."

"Have you already been for a run?" Darby asked, noticing that Megan wore sweats and carried a water bottle.

Megan usually stayed in bed until her mother shook her awake for school.

"I couldn't sleep," Megan said. She prowled the perimeter of Darby's room, but she didn't touch anything.

And that, Darby thought, was one of the traits that made Megan such a good friend. She might be nosy, but she wasn't pushy about it.

Darby stood up, took a deep breath, leaned over,

and touched her toes, then flipped her long black hair back like a mane.

"Better," she said. "I'm awake."

"Is this what you're wearing?" Megan stood in front of the white shirt and new jeans. "Where did you get this cool necklace?"

"Yeah, it's what I'm wearing," Darby said hesitantly. "But what necklace?" She didn't take a step closer. "The last time you talked to me about a necklace it was haunted or cursed or something."

"Stop it," Megan said, and though she was turned away and Darby couldn't see her face, she could hear the smile in her voice.

With delicate moves, Megan lifted a fine chain from the hanger and dangled it.

A winged gold heart the size of Darby's little fingernail swung back and forth before her eyes.

 Chapter Five

"It's beautiful, but it's not mine," Darby said, taking the necklace from Megan.

Then she recalled Jonah asking which jewelry she'd wear with the white blouse. And her mind replayed the hanger's clang when Jonah steered her back to bed at four A.M.

Megan took off her baseball cap, shook her hair loose, and waited for Darby to go on.

"Well, I guess it could be," Darby admitted. A heart with wings, though. She wasn't sure she understood. "Do you think Jonah gave it to me?"

"Stranger things have happened," Megan said. Tilting her head back, she drank the last of her water, then flashed an innocent smile. "I mean, you got your last jewelry from ancient ghosts."

"You know that still creeps me out," Darby said. "And I think that's something we won't share with my mom, if you don't mind."

Darby ran through her chores as fast as possible, but when she got back to Sun House, she could already hear Megan's hair dryer whining upstairs.

Hurry, she told herself. *You've got to look great.*

When she made it to the kitchen, she had every intention of just pouring a bowl of cereal and shoveling it down while standing at the counter.

"I need bigger calves," Jonah said. He and Aunty Cathy were dawdling over coffee as if it were an ordinary day. "I can't afford to ship them to the mainland for fattening, but this hippie grass-fed beef thing . . ."

What? Wasn't all beef grass fed?

Hurry. Don't listen to Jonah. Don't get into conversations that will make you late.

"Jonah, grass-fed beef is healthier," Aunty Cathy was saying.

"For cows or humans?"

"Both." Aunty Cathy looked serious. "And if there's one thing we have plenty of, it's grass. Besides," she added with a grin, "no one on earth would mistake you for a hippie."

Jonah's frown kept Darby from thanking him for the necklace. Besides, it could have been from Aunty Cathy. Even Megan could have slipped it in there and pretended to know nothing about it.

Why didn't she just ask? All at once, Darby realized her fingers felt cold. Before she'd come to Hawaii, that had only happened when she'd felt really unsure. On the verge of *timid*.

Darby blamed a combination of hurry and worry.

Vowing to shake off these feelings, she said the first thing that came into her head: "Did you ever have any paint horses?"

Before he answered, Jonah's eyes shifted toward the hallway. Something in the glance made Darby sure the necklace *had* been from him. But now he was answering her.

"If you mean your Tutu's Prettypaint, that mare's papers say she's a gray." He gave a long, dubious shrug. "I can't claim I'm unhappy to have her out of my sight, though."

"I think she's a beautiful horse." Aunty Cathy shot Darby a conspiratorial look.

"Me too," Darby said, but she hadn't been thinking of Prettypaint. She'd been picturing teenage Ellen, Ebony, a black-and-silver stallion, and the horse that had come to visit, just yesterday.

Darby took down a bowl and a box of cereal, then asked, "Don't you like paints?"

"Have I mentioned this is a Quarter Horse ranch? Seems like I did." Jonah used a knuckle to smooth one side of his mustache in mock concentration. "No wild *kanaka* stock from Crimson Vale or Sky Mountain, no blue-blooded Arabians, Thoroughbreds, Morgans, big-as-a-truck Friesians, or anything else."

"Okay," Darby said, trying not to spill the milk she was pouring.

"Just Quarter Horses. The registry won't accept paints, so I'm careful with my bloodlines." He glared at Aunty Cathy when she cleared her throat. "I'd never have one, and if some throwback popped up, I'd sell it."

Her mom had gone for revenge in a big way, then, Darby thought, but it didn't sound like she'd achieved it.

Darby finished her cereal just as Jonah started out of the kitchen and she was quick enough to catch him before he left the house.

"Thanks for the necklace," she said.

Her grandfather's wry smile said he wasn't surprised she'd read him like she did horses.

"It was just rattling around in a drawer," he said with a shrug, "but you're welcome."

"I really like it," she added.

"It's just a reminder," he said. The sun lines in Jonah's face turned downward as he laid his hands on her shoulders. "Your Hawaiian heart will always want to fly home."

Darby swallowed hard. Afraid she might cry if she tried to answer, she nodded over and over again until Jonah winked at her.

He left and she looked after him, but she was in such a hurry to get ready for the celebration, it was half an hour later, as she was blow-drying her hair, that Darby wondered why Jonah would have that pretty necklace just rattling around in a drawer.

Sugar Sands Cove Resort was crowded with cars.

Darby's friend Ann Potter waved as her father motioned Coach Roffmore into a parking space ahead of him. Miss Day swooped her bright yellow Volkswagen into a spot the coach had just given up on, and Jonah muttered in thanks when a hotel employee pointed out a place Aunt Babe had blocked off for Jonah, Cathy, Cade, Megan, and Darby.

"My guests of honor," Babe called. Her steps were rushed, and the rustling crush of a long white taffeta dress banded at the waist with a sash that matched her mango lipstick announced with every move that she was the hostess.

After Babe kissed all ten of their cheeks, she complimented her brother's paniolo finery and said, "You won't be sorry about those horses."

"We'll see," Jonah grumbled, but he kissed her cheeks in return.

Darby felt her eyes grow wide. That must mean Jonah had accepted Aunt Babe's gift of cremello horses, as an incentive to allow her guests to ride on 'Iolani Ranch. Guest riders would mean more money, but she had trouble picturing Jonah as a gracious host.

Aunt Babe escorted them into the hotel instead of allowing them to head toward the corral full of cremello horses, where a small stage had been erected.

Inside, there were white floors, mirrored walls, and transparent modern lamps filled with candles. Hotel guests twittered like excited birds, talking to reporters and each other as they savored the tropical perfumes of frangipani, ginger, and upright floral spears called birds-of-paradise.

"Watch your step." Aunt Babe pointed at cords snaking across the lobby floor. "We've got press everywhere."

Darby gazed after Aunty Cathy and Jonah as they stopped to talk to Kimo and an older man with sun-pleated skin and white hair. He must be Kimo's dad, Darby thought. Neck loaded with maile leis, he grinned and spoke in rapid-fire pidgin.

As he gestured, Darby noticed he was missing a finger. Was it really from a roping accident? Jonah and Kimo had told her, but Darby's head was spinning and she couldn't remember.

Deserted by her mother, Megan looked a little nervous, and that made Darby even more uneasy.

"We don't have to talk, do we?" Megan asked Aunt Babe. "We'll just sit in the crowd, the audience or whatever, with everyone else, then —"

"The chairs on the stage are for you," Aunt Babe explained.

"So, we'll just sit there and stand when you read off our names, but you'll do the talking?" Darby crossed all her fingers.

"Oh, no." Aunt Babe wagged a manicured nail. "This is small-town excitement at its best. But fun and wonderful publicity. Word's traveled about you brave kids, and the phone's still ringing. You three are going to sing for your supper."

"I can't sing," Cade insisted, shoving his hands into his pockets.

"It's just an expression," Darby told him. It would be rude to guess that Babe was reminding them publicity for the resort had been part of the agreement when they'd begun searching for the lost colt. Still, she turned to her great-aunt and said, "But if you really meant that, I'd skip supper."

Maybe Megan remembered she was the oldest, and, seeing there was no way out of this, she asked, "What do you want us to do?"

A movement outside caught Darby's attention. Mrs. Martindale and a man with salt-and-pepper hair, probably her husband, were waving, and Mark Larson, the TV reporter, was trying to get Aunt Babe's attention.

Kit and Cricket were there, too, checking out a long table of drinks and pastries, and Darby missed most of what Aunt Babe was saying until someone called Aunt Babe to the phone.

"While I take this call, why don't you go see Patrick. He'll help you with your leis." Aunt Babe paused to touch the gold chain of Darby's new necklace.

"Jonah gave it to me," Darby said. She hoped the

incredulity in her voice didn't sound rude.

Apparently Aunt Babe didn't think so.

"That's so nice. I'm sure you can arrange the lei so that it still shows."

Aunt Babe shooed them toward a gawky figure dressed in khaki slacks, a shirt buttoned to his chin, and glasses. Darby remembered seeing him at school and thinking he looked like Harry Potter.

Now, though, he stood in a mirrored corner that reflected the orange-and-purple birds-of-paradise flowers. Looking more like a fixture than a boy, he held out an arm draped with leis that gave off a wonderful scent.

"How're you doing, Patrick?" Megan asked.

"Good," Patrick said earnestly. "My septum wasn't fractured, after all."

Darby noticed the bandage under the nosepiece of his glasses, but she didn't ask what had happened because Jonah had returned to help them put on their leis.

If fresh ferns, honey, and baby powder could be fashioned into flowers, Darby thought as she put on the lei, they might smell like these blossoms, which Megan called pikake.

"Wonderful," said Aunt Babe, pointing at their leis as she stopped to talk to Mark Larson.

"I keep wondering if it was smart to sell that *keiki* a horse," Jonah muttered, with a glance at Patrick.

"He's totally accident prone," Megan explained in

a whisper. "Really smart and funny—in that Einstein kind of way—but watch for him at school and you'll see he always has an elastic bandage on his wrist or knee, or Band-Aids on his fingers."

"And what's his name?" Darby asked.

"Patrick Zink."

"Oh," Darby said. The only sign she'd ever seen of the Zinks, the family that shared a border with 'Iolani Ranch, was their barbed-wire fence.

"The way they let him play alone in the ruins of the old sugar mill, and along the pali," Jonah said, "it's amazing the kid's not dead."

"And you sold him a horse?" Darby asked.

"It was an ugly horse," Jonah said, shrugging. But when Darby didn't laugh, he looked annoyed. "You think he could hurt himself worse with a horse than runnin' around in that foggy old sugar plantation like he does?"

"No," Darby said, aghast, "but he could hurt the horse."

Jonah laughed, and so did Megan, and Darby guessed it was a little bit funny, but her mind was too fixated on her mother to laugh. Why wasn't Ellen here yet? Darby couldn't stop looking over her shoulder, searching for her mother.

Just then, she saw Aunt Babe ease away from Mark Larson and head back to them.

Behind her, Mark Larson studied his watch. Reporters had deadlines, Darby thought, and though she didn't see a clock anywhere, it must be getting awfully close to eleven o'clock. Where was her mom?

Aunt Babe's smile was brighter than before, as if she had news, but she just adjusted Cade's lei. "They look perfect," Aunt Babe said, patting Megan's shoulder. "And there's one left, for your mother," she told Darby. "That was her, calling from the airport in Hapuna! She tried you at the ranch, but of course you were already here. She's rented a car and she's on her way."

Darby barely suppressed a squeal of delight. Ellen Kealoha was back on Wild Horse Island!

It was almost an hour later when Aunt Babe gave in to a polite but pressured Mark Larson, and started the award ceremony before the arrival of Darby's mom.

The good thing about the delay was that Megan, Cade, and Darby had persuaded Aunt Babe to let them bring Stormbird up on the stage.

"He is the real star of the show," Megan insisted, and Aunt Babe was too busy to make much of a protest.

"Just walk him around now, and shake his sillies out so that he doesn't hurt himself up there, and *please*," she said, cupping Darby's cheek gently but insistently, "do not let him relieve himself in front of the cameras."

Now, the three teenagers stood in order of height — Megan, Cade, then Darby — next to each other, with

Stormbird in front of them.

The white colt leaned against their knees, watching the crowd with his turquoise eyes. Each time he tilted his head, snorted, or flicked his whisk of a tail, the "ahs" of the audience washed over Aunt Babe's storytelling.

From the small stage, Darby noticed that people in the audience kept looking back over their shoulders. Hoping to catch a glimpse of Ellen Kealoha, probably, but she still hadn't arrived.

Darby tried not to worry about her mom, as Aunt Babe explained how the three teenagers had tracked down Stormbird on the black sands of Night Digger Point Beach, how they'd lured him to safety by singing and offering him a wet bandanna to suck on. They got a standing ovation from the crowd, and Stormbird answered the clapping with a whinny.

Babe asked them all to stand, then come forward and say a few words as they received their checks.

Megan was great. Cherry Coke–colored hair glinting in the sun, she thanked Darby for spotting the colt in the first place and Cade for his paniolo expertise, then explained how she'd use her generous reward from Sugar Sands Cove Resort: for college, and to buy her mother a new set of sunflower-patterned dishes to replace those shattered by the earthquake.

Cade ducked his head, and talked so softly that Darby elbowed him.

"Say it again. Louder," she whispered.

He looked up and said, "I have to thank Mrs. Borden for payin' me for something I woulda done for nothin'."

Everyone must have heard him the second time, because they laughed and applauded. One woman — broad cheeked with lank blond hair — stood clapping after everyone else had stopped. She looked a little familiar, but Darby couldn't remember where she'd seen her before, and when she stood on tiptoe to get a better look at her, the woman shrank back into the crowd.

Then it was Darby's turn to speak.

Looking out over all the people made her feel dizzy, but she kept her hands on Stormbird's fluffy mane, and looked straight at Ann, pretending she was talking just to her.

"I guess I'm lucky, because I can say that Megan and Cade have already said what I wanted to." She paused, surprised at how many people were smiling. "Besides saving for college, I'm hoping to use some of my reward to fly my parents here so that they'll fall in love with Moku Lio Hihiu like I have."

Darby didn't know whether the applause was for what she'd said, or how she'd pronounced it, but she kept going.

"I'm really lucky that my mom and grandfather let me and my horse come here in the first place, and that Megan and Cade were willing to do this" — she nodded at Stormbird — "with me, a . . ." She took a deep breath and decided to risk more Hawaiian. "Um, *malihini*."

Cheers interrupted Darby, and the rows of warm-eyed smiles flashing her way made her feel less like a stranger than she had since she'd arrived.

Then, though she'd always been bad at conclusions—in both speeches and essays—she gave it a try.

"And I guess for once, I was in the wrong place at the right time, instead of the opposite."

"Whatever that means!" yelled Ann from the audience.

Darby took that as her cue to stop.

And she really would have, if people hadn't started talking and looking over their shoulders again.

Suddenly, Darby saw why they were chattering.

Everyone was staring at a beautiful woman in red high heels, but the woman was staring at *her*.

"Mom!" Darby shouted.

As Ellen Kealoha began working her way through the crowd, she blew Darby a kiss.

If it was possible to feel sunlight beaming from the inside out, Darby did.

 Chapter Six

Darby's joyous shout pretty much ended the award ceremony.

"Go ahead. Go see your mom." Megan gave Darby a nudge, then turned to Cade. "We'll take care of Stormbird, yeah?"

"Sure," Cade said.

"Thanks, you guys!" Darby said, then leaned over and kissed Stormbird between his oversize ears.

"Kiss the horse to thank us," Megan said, rolling her eyes, but Darby had already jumped off the stage.

Crab-stepping past a line of palm trees, Darby appeared right in her mother's path.

"You are gorgeous!" Ellen said, hugging Darby

and then holding her at arm's length.

Darby laughed. "I can breathe," Darby said, since her mom always worried about her asthma. "That helps, I guess."

"Let me look at you," her mom said. She spun one finger and Darby obeyed, turning around even though her boots hampered her twirl.

"Let's go over here," her mother said. Whisking Darby away from all those staring as if this were a performance, she guided her into a corner.

"I'm not as pale, am I?" Darby said when they stopped.

"In ten weeks . . ." Her mom shook her head. "Not pale, not weak, not bent over trying to drag in a breath."

For a second, Ellen's eyes filled with tears, reminding Darby how they'd sat in the car at the Los Angeles airport. *You'll love the ranch . . . you'll be in heaven . . . I'm not worried about you. . . .* But her mom had been worried.

"I got contact lenses, did I tell you?" Her mom fluttered her eyelashes, then squinted against her tears of relief, pretending she didn't quite recognize her daughter. "Still a bookworm?"

"Totally," Darby said. She rubbed her cheek, though the line from falling asleep on her book was long gone.

"Good," Mom said, and as her arms opened, Darby noticed her mom looked just like she always did—long black hair swooping against amber skin, sparkling almond-shaped eyes — but less tired. Less stressed.

The tropics agreed with Ellen. They were her home. And she looked more Hawaiian than ever as she kissed Darby's cheeks.

Inside their second hug, her mom whispered, "What about your huge reward?"

"A third of five thousand dollars," Darby whispered back, through a smile.

"A nice addition to your college fund," Ellen said, giving Darby an extra squeeze. "But you can spend a little of it if you do it wisely."

"I was going to spend it on your airfare. That's wise," Darby pointed out.

"Of course it is. I'm just lucky that our producer sprang for a weekend in Honolulu for the whole cast — because we're almost finished shooting — and all I paid for was the hop from there to Hapuna."

Darby didn't care about the details; she was just glad her mother was home.

"And how's Hoku?" her mom asked.

"You won't believe the difference in her. She's so smart. *Hapa kanaka*, that's what Jonah called her when —" Darby stopped, not ready to tell her mother about Hoku holding up a hitching rail so that it wouldn't crash down and hurt her. "She does this smart stuff," she finished lamely. "And she's beautiful. She's changed faster than I have."

"Cathy Kato sent me this." Ellen opened her small

clutch bag and showed her the photograph Aunty Cathy had taken of her riding Hoku. "It's a beautiful picture and you're every bit as pretty in person, and I bet Hoku is, too."

Darby straightened up. Her mom gazed at her as if she couldn't get enough, and even though it was a little embarrassing, Darby felt proud.

Her mother's gold hoop earrings danced when she shook her head as if she couldn't believe her eyes. Then she touched her forehead to her daughter's and said, "Let's go let your public congratulate you."

Tucked under her mother's arm for the next thirty minutes, Darby knew Ellen Kealoha was the unintentional star of the event.

Mark Larson had been on his way back to Channel Two when he recognized Ellen Kealoha speeding past him in her rented car. He'd made a U-turn and jumped out of the blue-and-orange van to trail after her.

Even though Ellen refused to give a press conference, saying the day belonged to the kids, the camera operator kept rolling as Babe dropped a pikake lei over Ellen's head and Ellen said, "I missed the turn, Aunty! Can you believe it? Everything's changed. The airport is like a real airport. The roads are paved, but I got lost!"

The roads weren't the only things that had changed since her mother had been gone. Darby looked around for her grandfather, but instead came face-to-face with

a woman she didn't recognize. She was chiding Aunt
Babe for keeping Ellen to herself.

As Mom caught up with developments in friends'
lives, Darby drifted away, but she still felt her mom
watching her, and Darby watched back. Their gazes
stayed locked on each other like magnets that pulled
apart, then rejoined.

Darby scanned the crowd again for Jonah. She
was ready to expand her search when she saw a silver dish mounded high with sugar cubes on the pastry
table.

Hoku had never tasted a sugar cube before. Darby
hesitated for a second, guessing sugar cubes were no
better for horses than they were for people, but figured one or two couldn't hurt, right? She slipped a
few into each of her front pockets. Navigator deserved
one, too. Then, giving up on the smooth fit of her new
jeans, she added a couple more, for Flight, Stormbird's
mother.

"I should have figured you were a thief, being from
Los Angeles."

Darby's hands were perched on her hips in outrage
when she turned to see that it was Duckie. Puzzled by
her cousin's vicious tone, as much as she was by the
accusation, Darby said, "I'm just getting a treat for the
horses. Aunt Babe wouldn't care, would she? Come
on. Let's ask."

"Never mind." Disgusted by Darby's unruffled
response, Duckie crossed her arms. Her lip poked out

like a sulky child's. "That'd be giving you what you want. You Kealohas just have to be the center of attention."

So that was Duckie's problem, Darby thought. She loved being in the spotlight, and today it just wasn't happening.

Tossing her metal-bright hair back over her shoulders, Duckie stalked away.

"Wow, how rude is that? Insulting your cousin and the entire city of Los Angeles?" Megan walked up with Ann and Cade.

"What was that about?" Ann asked.

"Sugar cubes," Darby said, looking after the tall girl.

"No worries." Ann tilted her head of red ringlets against Darby's shoulder, reassuring her, then said, "Hey, nice speech."

"I know, it was awful," Darby moaned.

"No, I meant it," Ann said, giving her friend a light punch. "You did great."

"You really did," Megan added. "That last part, where you said you were in the wrong place at the right time, was perfect. I mean, think of the volcano, the tsunami, the earthquake. Definitely wrong places, but you usually managed to make something good out of 'em."

"Thanks, Sis!" Darby said, surprised. Megan rarely sounded so thoughtful.

Brushing the compliment aside, Megan said,

"Introduce us to your mom."

"That might take a while." Ann nodded at the throng of people.

"This happen a lot?" Cade grimaced.

"Maybe it's because she hasn't been home in like fifteen years," Darby suggested.

"Her outfit . . ." Megan began, considering the stylish dress with slashes of black and white and the red hibiscus in her hair.

For the first time in hours, Darby thought of the black-and-white horse that had been hidden in the fold, but she put her equine questions aside as her mother laughed at something Aunt Babe had said.

"It's not the dress. It's my mom," Darby explained. "She'd wear those earrings and her hair loose like that to the grocery store," Darby said. Totally un-Hollywood, she thought. "And even those red shoes—"

"The heels aren't that high," Ann finished.

"They're hot," Megan judged as she edged closer to Ellen. Then, as if she had the peripheral vision of a horse, Megan snagged Cade's sleeve before he could escape the introduction to a celebrity. "Stop. I know Darby's mom wants to meet the paniolo who rescued her daughter."

Rescued me. Darby glared at Megan. *Oh yeah, let's take my happy mother and tell her stories about me risking my life all over the place.*

Her mom spun around, having overheard Megan.

"I certainly do!" she said.

Cade had just shaken off Megan's grip when the circle of people parted to include the teenagers.

"Mom, this is Cade. He . . ." Darby paused, not sure how to explain that Cade was sort of her hanai'd brother or cousin or something.

"I work on 'Iolani Ranch," Cade said quietly. "Aloha."

To Darby's amazement, Cade kissed Mom's cheeks in traditional welcome and she returned the gesture.

"You saved my daughter from drowning. I'll remember that always. *Mahalo*, Cade." Ellen's voice was as sincere as it was dramatic, so Darby didn't know why she felt compelled to break the silence that followed.

"Oh, heh, heh, you saw that? On television?" Darby asked. She heard the cartoon silliness in her laugh, but she couldn't help it.

"Oh, yes," her mom confirmed. She made her eyes feline narrow, as if to say, *You're in for it, now,* and added, "Tahiti does have television, you see."

But Darby could tell her mom wasn't playing. "It wasn't nearly as dangerous as it looked. I promise."

Ellen wasn't buying her casual attitude.

"Darby, dear, we'll talk about it later."

Darby, dear? She'd never heard those words paired before.

The entire news report unreeled in Darby's mind. So, she'd taken a risk riding into the floodwaters. On an untamed horse. To confront a villain like Manny. After a tsunami.

Darby drew a deep breath, but she didn't know what to say.

It had been *worse* than it had looked in a sixty-second news clip. Her mom would know that, and she'd know who to blame. Not just Darby, but Jonah.

With a silken voice and a glance toward Mark Larson, this time it was Aunt Babe who came to Darby's rescue. And she did it by changing the subject.

"Ellen, do tell us all about the new film that brought you to our part of the world."

"Brought her home," Darby corrected, but her mom pretended not to hear.

Darby stepped backward and bumped into Stormbird, Megan, and Ann. Both girls looked at her askance, but Stormbird just snuffled her pocket, and Cade considered the ground, hands in his own pockets, doing his best to disappear.

"What's wrong?" Darby hissed.

"Don't start grinding on her yet," Ann told Darby.

"What?" Darby was amazed at the warning in Ann's tone.

"Your mom. I know you want to smooth things out between her and Jonah, and I know you want to stay here with Hoku—"

"And we *want* you to stay," Megan added.

"—but just hang back for a little while," Ann concluded.

Ellen's voice floated over her ring of admirers.

". . . not exactly on Easy Street, but things are going well enough that Darby and I will be able to flee the suburbs for the city. I've got my eye on a high-rise apartment with a view of the Hollywood hills. . . ."

Aunt Babe must have felt Darby's alarm, because she slid her a calming look. It didn't work. A sickening sweet smell welled up from Aunt Babe's orchid lei. Darby felt light-headed, as if she were falling toward the flowers' peach-streaked throats.

Ann brushed Darby's hair away from her ear.

"I know what I'm talking about," Ann whispered. "If you take her on here and now, you'll lose."

"That goes for Jonah, too," Megan insisted, because Darby's grandfather had just stepped into view. He looked toward Ellen, shading his eyes. "Right, Cade?"

When Cade shrugged, Megan leaned toward him, nose to nose.

"I know you agree."

Cade looked down at his boots. He showed no sign of the confident kid he'd been last night, until Megan rephrased her question.

"Cade, what would you say to Jonah if you were in Darby's place right now?"

Cade slid his hand under his paniolo braid and rubbed the back of his neck.

"Nothin', just . . . nothin'." But then he looked up. His brown eyes met Darby's. "Don't saddle 'em up and make 'em prance for you, yeah? Not yet. Give 'em some time."

Darby was pretty sure she understood, and though Megan and Ann looked dubious, they both said, "See?"

Darby sighed. Her friends cared about her. They thought they knew best, and maybe they did.

But Darby's mind wouldn't stop replaying something *she* knew.

In the city there'd be no place for a wild horse.

Chapter Seven

With his deadline looming, Mark Larson finally left the celebration, but he'd extracted a promise from Ellen Kealoha to do a full interview the next time she visited Moku Lio Hihiu.

As the reporter departed, Darby saw Jonah stroll toward the corral of cremellos.

It was just like Jonah to be invisible until the TV crew had left. Darby couldn't blame him for not wanting a reunion—especially one this uncertain—to be shown on television.

Most people knew the Kealohas' story already. Generations of "secrets" were confided and discussed on the small island, but Jonah had spotted a place where they might still have some privacy.

Earlier, visitors had admired the herd of cream-colored horses, but now most people were leaving for home or drifting past the corral to walk on the resort's famed white-sand beach.

Megan must have seen Jonah, too, because she thrust Stormbird's halter rope at Darby and said, "He's sleepy and hungry. Could you take him back to Flight?"

Darby would have pushed the chore onto Cade, but he was nowhere in sight. All at once Darby realized the woman she had not quite recognized in the crowd could have been Cade's mother, Dee. Could Cade be with her?

Megan and Ann disappeared before Darby could ask, and since Stormbird was sucking on her fingers, underlining his need for a snack, Darby turned to her mother.

"Mom, would you like to see Stormbird's mother, Flight? And the rest of Aunt Babe's cremello horses?"

"I'd love to! I don't know anything about cremellos," her mom said, following in her clacking heels while Darby told her all she could remember.

Aunt Babe came with them, filling in the gaps, then added, "Did you know my stubborn brother finally agreed to take the cremellos?"

"I heard him say something that made me think so," Darby said wonderingly.

Ellen gazed at the herd of ivory horses up ahead.

"He didn't want them." Ellen's tone was flat, but one corner of her mouth quirked up as if she weren't surprised.

"It's not that he didn't want them," Darby spoke up. "He's just not too crazy about having tourists on the place. At least, that's what I think."

"You're right," Aunt Babe agreed. "And Jonah's doing me a favor by taking them."

"No piling on," Ellen said, holding up her hands. Her tone was amused, but her lips tightened and it was clear she felt her daughter and aunt were defending Jonah.

"Except for these two," Aunt Babe said. Ignoring her niece's remark to talk about her horses, she rubbed the poll Flight offered for attention. "Flight and Stormbird will have a home here as long as I live."

All at once Darby remembered the sugar cubes. She dug into her pocket and had barely flattened her palm with the cube in the center of it when the cremellos moved like a flock of gulls in her direction.

"Now what?" Darby yelped.

Her mother and great-aunt laughed and helped her share all but two of the cubes with the horses. As Darby lectured one especially pushy horse about rudeness, her mother shook her head and said, "I wish your father could be here, baby. He told me to tell you he's proud."

"About what?" Darby asked.

"Everything! You have taken some big steps

toward growing up." Ellen sniffed, sighed, and patted Darby's cheek before she added, "This is no time to get sentimental."

Ellen looked across the corral and Darby saw her shiver.

Jonah shaded his eyes as if looking into the sun, but the sun was behind him. He squinted, then strode toward them from around the corral, looking proud of his daughter, too.

It's going to be okay, Darby thought.

Jonah and Ellen mirrored each other. Their smiles were shaky. Their arms reached out. Darby saw how they'd missed each other.

But then, pride interfered. Darby saw it happen.

Pride reminded Ellen her acting career would have gotten off to an earlier start, if not for her father.

Pride took Jonah back to the lonely years after his wife died, after his daughter was gone. And pride reminded him that Ellen had run away. She'd abandoned him on purpose.

Father and daughter looked stiff, and there was hesitation as they kissed each other's cheeks. But when they hugged, their hands pressed and patted each other's backs, and Darby's hope flickered back to life.

Love was hard to snuff out.

"It's good to see you," Ellen said.

"And you," Jonah replied, then cleared his throat and rushed his words. "You'll—*will* you come to the house for a late lunch, and maybe a ride?"

He'd changed his demand into a request. Darby hoped her mother had noticed.

"Please, Mom!" Darby bounced up and down, then tugged at her mother's arm. Acting like a three-year-old didn't fit with the advice she'd gotten from her friends, but she couldn't help it. "You have to see Hoku. Please?"

"Yes, to the lunch — Cathy already invited me — and *maybe* to the ride," Ellen said.

"Let's go," Darby said. She couldn't give her mother time to change her mind, so she turned politely to Aunt Babe. "Thanks so much for everything. . . ."

"Not just this minute," Ellen cautioned Darby. Then she glanced to Jonah.

Why? Darby wondered. Was her mother asking for Jonah to help?

"You two work it out," Jonah said, then turned away and headed for the parking lot.

"You know I'm staying here with Aunty Babe," her mom said gently.

"I — no, I didn't." Darby drew the words out, trying to overrule her panic with logic.

She reviewed beds and bedrooms at the ranch. Unless she and Mom shared her bed or they made up the couch with sheets and blankets, there was no obvious place for Ellen to sleep.

Could Ellen remember how much she loved the ranch if she only came for lunch?

"I'd love to have Darby stay here, too," Aunt Babe urged.

Darby couldn't think of anything to say that wouldn't make her sound ungrateful.

"We'll see about that, but right now Hoku needs you. Am I right?" Ellen asked. "And Aunt Babe has some people she'd like me to meet, so we'll just split up for an hour or so. It's the least I can do, since I took a loan from Aunty and never paid her back." Ellen turned to Aunt Babe. "Don't think I've forgotten."

"And *you*, don't be silly! The first time I saw your face on my television screen, I was repaid. And when I saw your wedding pictures. And that adorable Mamma Mia photograph!"

Her mom laughed, then turned toward Darby. But Ellen didn't have to explain it.

"I know which picture she means," Darby said. "That old one from the newspaper? Where you and Dad are standing in front of a big oven and Dad's holding a pizza and you're wearing a checked apron with, uh, me pooching it out?"

"That's the one!" Aunt Babe said.

"It's still on the restaurant wall," Darby said, and suddenly she smelled the yeasty dough, thick red sauce, and gooey cheese of her father's Italian restaurant back in California.

"I miss Dad," Darby said.

"You miss pizza," her mom corrected her.

"*And* Dad," Darby said. "Do you think they'd come over to visit?"

Skepticism glittered in her mom's dark eyes. Darby didn't know what it meant until Ellen asked, "Would *you* travel with five children under ten years old?"

Before anyone answered with more than a smile, Ellen gave Darby a gentle swat on the seat of her jeans. "Your grandfather's waiting for you," she said, pointing toward the truck.

Darby leaned her head against her mother's shoulder and closed her eyes. Her mind knew she was only leaving for an hour or two, but her heart hurt at the thought of going away.

Ellen's arms closed around Darby in a hug before she kissed the top of her hair and said, "I'll be along soon."

At last, Darby left. It was a good thing, too, since everyone else was already in the truck. Jonah and Aunty Cathy sat up front. Darby climbed into the backseat with Cade and Megan.

Aunty Cathy had plenty of compliments for Cade, Darby, and Megan on the ride home, and some for Ellen, too, but Darby hardly listened.

"It's cool that she's coming for lunch," Megan said.

Darby was so preoccupied with planning a persuasive afternoon with her mother, she didn't hear what was on the menu.

But when they reached the ranch, Aunty Cathy touched Darby's arm to get her attention. "Why don't you go ahead and change into riding clothes and grab a quick snack."

"But—"

"Your aunt Babe might hang on to your mother for a while, now that she's got her hands on her."

Darby changed into an everyday T-shirt—a newish yellow one her mom had never seen—but she left on her good jeans and boots and headed for Hoku's corral. Maybe she'd get Cade or Kit to show her that bronc stop that Jonah had mentioned. Maybe she'd be riding Hoku when her mom arrived. Mane, tail, and ponytail flowing, they'd be rocking in Hoku's smooth lope, looking so perfect together that her mom would give up dreams of city apartments.

But Kit couldn't show her the bronc stop.

He'd ridden out with Kimo to repair a watering trough that had loosened in the soggy ground, then tipped over. Jonah was riding Kona, smoothing the gelding out, Cade said, in case Ellen wanted to ride him.

It seemed to Darby that the cowboys had left Cade behind with nothing to do except give her a hard time.

"Do you want to start me and Hoku on the bronc stop?" Darby asked.

"I think you should groom her instead."

"But I want to be riding when my mom gets here. The last time she saw Hoku, she was sick and lying in a stall."

"Those early-morning showers made her feet muddy.

And the end of her tail, a little," Cade pointed out.

"Okay, but the main thing is —"

"She'd enjoy the massage," Cade said.

"What's going on? Why don't you want me to ride?" Darby studied Cade's expression, but his brown eyes gave her no hints. "Do you just want to keep your paniolo tricks to yourself?"

"You're too *pupule* just now to try bronc stoppin'," Cade said.

"What?" Darby demanded. "I'm not crazy."

"Wound up," Cade tried again. "Kind of hyper because . . . you know."

Darby *did* know, and Cade was right. Her excitement would telegraph to her horse and, not knowing why Darby was jittery, Hoku might respond with agitation of her own.

Darby sighed. She retrieved Hoku's halter and orange-striped lead rope from the tack room and asked, "So, you think this will settle us both down?"

"Yes, ma'am." Cade gave a perfect imitation of Kit's buckaroo drawl, and Darby guessed the intensive grooming session had probably been the foreman's idea.

"All right," Darby conceded.

Although grooming a horse kept on rain-washed grass wasn't as important as a horse kept in a stall, Jonah had told Darby it was an important part of the gentling process for Hoku. After her injury, grooming had acted as a massage for the wild filly and helped

Darby keep dust and bugs away from her wounds.

"Come on, my beautiful girl," Darby told Hoku.

Darby thought the filly was lowering her head for the halter until she realized the mustang was sniffing her pocket. Hoku had scented the sugar.

"You've never had this, have you?" Darby mumbled, working her fingers into her pocket. "Two left," she said. As she withdrew the sugar, Hoku nudged her hand with loud snuffling. "One for each of us."

Darby popped a sugar cube into her mouth, then flattened her palm. Hoku took another loud breath, lipped at the white cube, and knocked it off Darby's hand.

The sugar was melting on Darby's tongue by the time Hoku nibbled the sugar cube, raised her head, tilted it back, and crunched. For an instant, the filly's eyes closed, and then saliva dripped from her mouth to the white star on her chest.

"Pretty good, huh?" Darby asked. Hoku tossed her head up and down in agreement and Darby wished she'd given her both treats.

After Hoku was haltered, Darby led her from the corral. She concentrated on tying a quick-release knot that would please Cade's watchful eyes and keep Hoku safe.

She passed the rope through the ring, forming a sort of bow, and pulled the bow tight.

"Put that loose end through, too," Cade reminded her.

Hoku flattened her ears, telling him to go away, but Darby just said, "So it can't be undone, I know."

"Up to you," Cade said with a shrug. "Kimo thinks she's figuring out how to let herself go."

That's just what we need, Darby thought, *for Mom to arrive and find me gone on a wild horse chase.* So she poked the loose end through, where it would be hard for fluttering lips to grab and teeth to jerk.

After that, Darby felt her way down her horse's leg, speaking gently, then picked out Hoku's feet from heel to toe. Darby smiled at the squishy sound of Hoku's tongue searching her mouth for every last grain of sugar.

With the filly's feet done, Darby faced her into the wind to use the curry comb. Hoku's winter coat was nearly gone, but she didn't want any loose hair or dust to blow into the mustang's eyes.

Last, she sprayed hair conditioner on Hoku's mane and tail and worked the milky solution through. She'd started using her fingers to untangle knots ever since she'd seen Megan do it with her rose roan Tango.

"Prevents breakage and split ends," Megan had insisted, like a hairstylist.

Besides, Darby thought, this way didn't pull as much and Hoku didn't flinch.

"You could rub a little baby oil on her face," Cade suggested. "It'd look real pretty."

"How long do you plan to keep me occupied?" Darby asked.

Cade glanced toward the ranch road, then shrugged. "Long as it takes, I guess."

Just then, the high-low call of a turkey was answered by others of its kind. Darby listened as intently as her horse.

A rafter of turkeys, Darby thought. She'd read that's what they were properly called, instead of a covey, like quail, or a flock, like geese.

But she didn't share this information with Cade. Instead, she thought of the tumbling gray-brown chicks that would be following the turkey hens.

"Hey! Did you see your mom at the—"

Cut off by Cade's intent look, Darby just gestured toward the resort.

"Did *you* see her?" he asked.

"Well, that's what I mean. *I* wouldn't recognize her, because I've only seen her once before on TV, but this lady—while you were talking . . ." Darby wasn't sure how to describe the look in the woman's eyes. Cade might think she was being *sentimental*, to use Mom's word, or *pupule*, to use his own.

But maybe not. All at once Darby understood the expression of someone "hanging on" the words of another.

"Go ahead." Cade's voice was almost a whisper, and Darby kicked herself for bringing this up when she wasn't sure.

What if Dee had left the island? No one had seen Cade's mother since the tsunami.

Trying not to give Cade false hope, Darby went on, "I just thought it might be her because of the way she was looking at you while you were standing up, talking. She looked *satisfied*. Like everyone was giving you what you deserved, or something."

Cade's face looked happy and sad at the same time. And then he walked away.

"Okay," Darby said to Hoku as she watched Cade go. "That went really well, didn't it?"

She pressed her cheek against Hoku's silky neck.

Eyes closed, Darby heard Cade's boots climb the stairs up to the porch, then go into the bunkhouse. He returned right away, and Darby stepped back from her horse.

"Here," Cade said. He held out a tattered photo. "Is that her?"

In the picture, Cade was a gap-toothed toddler straddling the shoulders of a grinning woman. Tall, with a face round as the body of a banjo and gleaming blond hair, she steadied Cade's leg with one hand and his shoulders with the other.

So careful, Darby thought. *What changed?*

 Chapter Eight

Darby stared at the photograph of Cade and his mother while Cade waited. He was patient, giving her time to think about it.

Even if she told herself the photograph had been taken twelve or so years and an emotional lifetime ago, Darby wasn't sure.

"I can't tell," Darby said. "I'm sorry, Cade."

"Yeah, well," Cade said, and he left, taking the photograph back inside.

"No sign of *your* mom yet?"

Darby jumped at the voice behind her. She'd been concentrating so hard, she'd missed Megan's approach.

"Not yet," she said, and Darby suddenly felt thankful.

What if she'd been born to Dee instead of Ellen Kealoha? She'd done nothing to deserve good parents. Cade had done nothing to deserve a mother who had looked the other way when he was being beaten by his stepdad.

Her own mother would never put her second to anyone. Darby knew it with every molecule of her being.

Cade's face was blank as he came back down the steps from the bunkhouse porch, but Darby wished she'd kept the sighting to herself.

She felt another twinge of guilt when gravel crunched under the tires of her mother's watermelon-colored rental car.

"Hey," Cade said to Darby.

When Darby looked at him, Cade shook his head and winked as if he were giving her the go-ahead to celebrate.

Ellen drove so slowly down the ranch road, head swinging to stare from her windows, that the rental car didn't raise dust, and Peach and Bart, the two Australian shepherds that hadn't romped off to the pastures with Kimo and Kit, didn't bark.

Curious sentries, the dogs stood with ears pricked toward the car and tails fanning at half-mast.

"Guess they recognize family," Megan said, patting Peach's head as she and Darby went past to greet Darby's mom.

Darby had assumed Aunt Babe would further stake her claim on Ellen by driving her mother to the ranch. But her mom had come alone, and even though she still wore high heels and a stylish dress, Ellen popped out of the car with her eyes and arms wide, as if she'd embrace everything around her.

"Oh, Darby, we *are* going riding. I have places and things to show you! Do I ever!" When the wind flared her skirt, Ellen pushed it down absentmindedly, then stared off the bluff, toward the rain forest. "And Tutu, let's visit her as well, shall we?"

Bart and Peach rushed to Ellen, and though Cade snapped, "Steady," ordering them to calm down, the Australian shepherds nuzzled and licked Ellen's offered hands before they obeyed.

Darby's mom loved the ranch. Her perfectly applied cosmetics couldn't hide the joy that glowed on her face.

Darby was only a millisecond away from throwing herself into her mother's arms again when the shamble of hooves drew her attention as Jonah pulled Kona to a stop out by the tack shed and yelled, "Pig scraps."

An instant after he said it, Jonah started as if he'd just noticed the rental car, and then his daughter.

"Aloha," he said.

Something in Jonah's tone confused Darby. He sounded almost like Ellen had pulled a trick on him. Had he expected her to come later, or what?

"Almost time for lunch." Jonah sounded merely matter-of-fact as he dismounted, loosened Kona's saddle cinch, then went into the tack shed.

Ellen's elation had faded.

"No big deal," Darby said. She laughed, trying not to analyze her mother's expression. It wasn't sympathy or disgust. "Ever since I adopted a new piglet, it's my job to slop the hogs. And feeding the animals is more fun than doing dishes or cleaning my room."

Every word was true, but couldn't Jonah have reminded her before her mom got here or after she'd left?

"I'll do it. You can pay me back," Megan said. She darted toward the house for the bucket.

"Thanks!" Darby called after her. "Mom, come see Hoku. You won't believe your eyes."

"Wait," Ellen said, before Darby could lead the way. "I'll go see her after lunch. No pouting. It's just that I didn't bring riding clothes because I had no idea I'd want to go riding. But I've changed my mind. I can't wait."

"You and Aunty Cathy are about the same size," Darby suggested.

"Exactly what I was thinking." Her mom looked as if she were about to ask a question when Darby cut her off.

"Okay, but can't you just come look at her?"

Her mom was using both index fingers to point down at her red high heels when the chinging of Jonah's spurs made them look up.

"How'd that happen?" Jonah asked, looking at Ellen's feet.

"I guess the ranch girl turned into a city girl," Ellen said coolly. "It happens."

"And vice versa." Jonah nodded at Darby.

Don't put me in the middle of this, Darby thought, but it was too late.

"There's a difference between a ranch girl and an unsupervised child allowed to run wild and get into life-threatening situations," her mom snapped.

"Mom." Darby gasped.

"I only want what's best for you, and that starts with keeping you safe."

Her mom's honesty was obvious and not overshadowed by a grudge.

"Lunch!" Megan yelled as she trotted past with a bucket. "Oh, for us, too, my mother said. I'll be right back."

Unsupervised child.

Running wild.

Life-threatening situations.

Okay, Darby thought as she helped Aunty Cathy carry lunch out onto the lanai, the last one was valid, but Jonah didn't deserve the blame.

Hundreds of people on the island—hadn't Tutu said something like it was a young land, still forming?—had felt the earthquake and been endangered by the tsunami.

Aunty Cathy carried a sizzling metal platter of steaks onto the lanai. Darby was about to follow with a basket of rolls and homemade french fries when Megan, carrying a bowl of fruit salad, bumped her hip against Darby's.

"What now?" Darby grumbled.

"Don't brood, or you'll blow it."

"Girls?" Aunty Cathy called.

Darby exhaled. She pictured herself flouncing onto the lanai with the hatboxes and presenting her mother with her past. She knew her mother well enough to think Ellen would be embarrassed at the hint she was still acting like a defiant teenager. Sort of.

"Knock it off," Megan said. "They'll work it out."

"What? Now I can't even sigh?"

"That wasn't a sigh. It was a huff," Megan told her. "And I ought to know."

Darby chuckled, bumped Megan back, and hoped for the hundredth time that 'Iolani Ranch would remain her home.

Ellen and Jonah left their quarrel out in the ranch yard. Aunty Cathy and Ellen got along so well—talking about cooking, clothes, movies, and weather—it was hard to believe they'd never met before today.

"I knew Ben," her mom said. She'd reached between the pitchers of tea and lemonade to lay her hand atop Aunty Cathy's, but she looked at Megan. "He saved me lots of broken bones, I'll tell you."

There was a Hawaiian cadence and kindness in Ellen's voice, then, that made everyone love her back.

"Thanks. Me too." Megan cleared her throat.

Then, with a trembling smile, she changed the subject. "I want to know all about being an actress. It sounds so glamorous."

"I adore acting," Ellen said in a qualified way. "But times haven't always been easy. . . ."

"You didn't have to make them so hard," Jonah put in as he popped a french fry into his mouth.

Ellen's glassy smile stayed in place as she continued, "Because I knew nothing but this ranch. I had to teach myself everything else."

"There's no pleasing this one," Jonah said. He turned his gaze from Ellen to Cathy. "I kept her safe at home and she ran away. I give my granddaughter the freedom her mother was champing at the bit to have, and that's no good, either."

"There's a big difference between freedom and . . ." Ellen let her voice trail off as if she'd promised herself that she wouldn't be drawn into another quarrel. Blotting her lips with her napkin, she turned to Cathy and said, "I saw her on television."

They were both looking at Cathy and both their voices were too level.

"You sent her to me a timid little mouse. Not a daredevil like her mother. Good sense tempered her horse craziness, most of the—" Jonah stopped and tapped the table with his fist. "She's doing fine." He kept tapping, and water lapped over the edge of Darby's glass. "Fine."

Megan sat back in her chair. Aunty Cathy dabbed

up the drop of water. Ellen watched Darby as if she had the answer to a riddle, but no one stormed away from the table.

Jonah's eyebrows lined up straight across his forehead as he studied Darby. "I'm doing better with this one, and she's doin' good enough to run this ranch." He ignored the gasps all around him. One of them might even have come from Darby herself.

"That's not happening, Jonah," Ellen said softly.

Darby remembered thinking her mother would never put her second. Not to a man like Manny, and not as the bone of contention in a feud with her father, either, right?

Jonah pretended not to hear Ellen. He picked up Darby's hand and touched the calluses on her palm and the scraped knuckles on her fingers.

He gave a firm nod. "Not next week, you know. But eventually."

For a minute it was so quiet, Darby heard the dogs yapping and running in a game of chase in the ranch yard. Francie's chain clinked as she grazed in the shade. A faucet dripped in the kitchen.

"I'll go turn that off," Megan said, and Darby didn't blame her for grabbing the excuse to escape as Ellen took a loud breath, looking like she'd just gotten her second wind to continue the fight.

"Tell her," Aunty Cathy said. There was no doubt she was addressing Jonah.

"Tell me what?" Ellen asked.

"Nothing," Jonah said, pushing back from the table.

"Jonah." Cathy's tone was either a warning or a plea.

"Nothing," he repeated. "At least, nothing to do with you. Now, are you going to go ride, or shall I put that horse up? That Kona? He's brother to your Pretty-paint. She's a gray." Jonah said it with as much certainty as he'd use telling her that 'Iolani Ranch grew green grass.

"I want to ride," Ellen said.

Then Aunty Cathy offered to loan Ellen boots and jeans and showed her where she could change.

Glad that she'd be riding out on horseback with her mother for the first time ever, Darby still kept wondering what secret Aunty Cathy and Jonah were keeping.

Tell her. Judging by Aunty Cathy's voice, it wasn't a happy secret. And her mom's reaction indicated she was afraid of the same thing, because Darby had heard a quaver in her mother's voice when she'd asked, *Tell me what?*

Chapter Nine

Darby and her mother walked down to see Hoku after Ellen changed into borrowed riding clothes. Halfway to the corral, Ellen stopped looking around as if she could soak up the scenery of home, and touched Darby's new necklace.

"That's cute," she said. "Where did you get it?"

Darby touched the gold flying heart. "I've kind of been thinking it used to be yours, since Jonah gave it to me."

Her mother's black eyebrows arched in surprise before she said, "Not mine."

"He said it would remind me that my Hawaiian heart would always want to fly home," Darby said. She winced because she'd mangled Jonah's words, but her mother seemed to understand, anyway.

"He loves you," Ellen said.

Darby didn't know what to say.

Hoku interrupted with a quivering neigh.

"So does she." Ellen nodded at Hoku.

The filly stopped trotting toward the fence. She danced in place when she realized the stranger meant to keep coming closer.

"And so do I," her mother said, giving Darby's shoulders a squeeze. "And, oh, honey—" Darby's mother broke off as if Hoku had stolen her breath. "She's exquisite."

The late-spring sun turned the filly's coat to copper fire, and her mane floated around her.

Ellen sounded as if she couldn't believe her eyes, and now, knowing her mother had been raised as a horsewoman—she hadn't known that when her mother had admired Hoku in the cold Nevada barn months ago—Darby smiled with pleasure.

"Before, when she was at Mrs. Allen's horse sanctuary," Ellen went on, "I could see what she'd been and how much she'd taken to you, but her coat was dull and stiff, and so were her eyes. She had sunken places over her eyes, too, as if she was a very old horse."

"She was traumatized," Darby explained as she offered her hand over the top of the fence, coaxing her horse to come closer.

"You fixed that," Ellen said, and then, noticing the bruise across the back of her hand, she asked,

"But who fixes you?"

Darby turned her hand palm up, hiding the spot where the lead rope had pulled tight.

"What did you do? That must have hurt," her mother said. "I've always heard people bruise where they have fat, and your hands are nothing but skin and bones."

Before Ellen could press her further for an answer, Hoku walked within about five feet of the fence and studied Ellen.

Chin tucked against her neck, Hoku gazed through her eyelashes as intently as if she were looking over the top of spectacles.

Ellen laughed. "Come here, my lovely."

Hoku did, accepting the touch of her human's mother, and feeling the kindness in her hands.

Darby and her mother had been riding for nearly an hour when they saw a ring of clouds around the top of the ohia trees. Then a coasting owl pulled a gray shawl of rain in its wake. As they rode through a corridor of trees so straight it must have been planted by humans, the fog crashed over the forest before them like a wave, and pressed close, filling every unoccupied space with spun-silver moisture.

"It's like riding back in time," Ellen whispered.

"Into a cloud forest," Darby agreed.

Bird calls could be screeching dinosaurs, Darby thought. Wild Horse Island could be rising from an

ancient bog on a world so new it was still being shaped
by volcanoes and the sea. This fog was far different
from the lung-eating volcanic vapors that had choked
her just weeks ago. This fog smelled of woodland
earth, fern fronds, and salt.

Navigator's hooves thudded beneath her, but
Darby couldn't hear Kona's hoofbeats. The fog blot-
ted out sound, along with scenery.

Muffled senses would usually have made Darby
nervous, but her mom had grown up here and they
rode side by side, partners in a primeval world.

Questions swirled in Darby's mind, but she
refused to break this spell. In the saddle, her mother's
grace and fluid strength told Kona not to question her
as she'd set him into step beside Navigator. Why had
Ellen ever stopped riding?

Her mom couldn't hide her passion for the island's
emerald hills and crystal air. She trotted into veils of
mist with her face thrust forward, absorbing its magic.
So why had she ever left?

Ellen couldn't stop praising Darby's new health,
prettiness, and her ease with the huge bay Navigator. Watching Darby swing into the saddle and settle there, her mother had folded her fingers together
almost prayerfully, and held them against her mouth
as she murmured, "Oh, look at you!"

Now, Navigator snorted an inquiry and Kona
halted. Navigator stepped between the smaller horse
and the rustling foliage on their right. Ears alert, both

animals stared as if their equine eyes pierced the fog.

"What do you think it is?" Ellen leaned forward on Kona's neck, sounding eager.

She wouldn't sound so jolly if she'd been dodging rabid hogs, Darby thought.

But this wasn't the sound of rooting; it was—

"A horse," Darby suggested.

As if she'd said abracadabra, a breeze parted the mist to show a black-and-white horse standing a few feet off the trail.

"Ohhh . . ." Ellen's delighted sigh matched Darby's.

Masked by satiny black from muzzle to eye patches, the horse studied them. Its flat cheeks, forehead, and neck were white, but a black swan's throat flowed down to the ferns among which she stood. All they could see of the rest of the horse was a black mane blowing in inky tendrils.

"I know that horse. . . ." Ellen shivered in recognition.

"So do I," Darby said, but she didn't tell her mother that the horse had appeared at the fold yesterday. Instead, the words of her mother's diary echoed in Darby's memory.

He came for Ebony, a wild black-and-white paint stallion.

Her mother's lips parted in amazement, but she didn't speak.

"You're tame, aren't you?" Darby asked the paint as it touched noses with Navigator and Kona.

Tame and friendly, just as she had been with Hoku yesterday, Darby thought. Remembering how her reach for the lead rope had frightened the horse yesterday, Darby didn't move.

But then the horse rubbed her dew-beaded whiskers on Ellen's forearm.

"I guess I can see who's her favorite," Darby said, pretending to pout.

"You stepped out of my dreams, didn't you?" Ellen's fingers touched the tracery of veins under black-and-white skin. "When I was a girl, I saw a horse like this, a wild paint stallion."

Darby knew the story from her mother's diary, but she let Ellen tell it just the same.

"Even though Jonah hated paints and wouldn't have a non–Quarter Horse on the place, I let down the rails on my mare's corral — her name was Ebony — and hoped she'd have a foal that looked just like this."

"Did she?" Darby asked.

"No," her mom said, sighing. "She had a black filly, probably Luna's, and I think we named her Crow — no, Raven. Moon Raven, or something like that. I didn't get to know her very well."

Darby would have thought her mom's daring had amounted to nothing more than a prank, if the black-and-white mare hadn't stood before them.

"This is the horse I wanted to be born." Darby's mom continued as she turned to look at her. "Are you surprised your mother was such a bad kid?"

Darby smiled. She couldn't admit that the shock had worn off after twenty-four hours, so she said, "Kinda."

"So am I," Ellen said. "Today at lunch, I was braced against the table arguing with Jonah like we'd never stopped. But this time I'm fighting for you."

"I—you don't have to, not about this," Darby said.

"Honey, ranching will break your heart," her mother said.

"I don't care," Darby said. And her mother must have heard her conviction, because they both watched the beautiful horse in silence as it inspected the saddle horses.

The paint moved along Kona's left side, walked behind the two geldings, then bumped Darby's right stirrup before disappearing back into the foliage.

"Have you ever seen her before?" Ellen asked.

"Yes, but I thought she was wild, from the Crimson Vale herd. Their leader is Black Lava, a black with one blue eye. Actually, he *was* in Crimson Vale, but he's penned up on the Lehua High School football field now."

"Really? Why?" her mother asked, and then she seemed to remember what she'd seen on television. "Oh, that's where they funneled them to, after you and Cade and Kit—"

"Yeah," Darby interrupted. She didn't want her mom worrying over the tsunami again. As a distraction, she grasped onto something her mother had mentioned earlier. "When you mentioned Luna, that was Old Luna, right?"

"Big bay stallion? He's the only Luna I know." She shrugged.

"About five years ago, Black Lava killed him."

Ellen winced.

"Jonah tried to shoot Black Lava, but he only wounded him."

"He missed," Ellen said in a wondering tone.

"Yeah, and when he finally found him in the forest, the stallion was down, and Jonah decided not to kill him. He just marked his hoof, so that if he came back, he could finish the job."

A gust of wind startled a scarlet bird on the twig overhead. He gripped tighter, then gave up and flew away.

"When did Jonah get so big on second chances?" Ellen asked, and she didn't sound a bit sarcastic.

"I don't know," Darby said. "We still have Old Luna's son. He's the ranch stallion now."

"Good," her mother said, then added, "What I said about Jonah and second chances . . . I'm not complaining. It's just that he was never like that before. Before, it was 'what I say goes.'"

"He's still pretty much that way," Darby said. "My very first day on the ranch, before I even knew who he was, he told me not to pet the horses."

Her mom didn't look surprised, but then the wild

cane plants rustled and an eerie howl came from the forest. Instead of looking scared or even startled, her mother let out a delighted cry.

"It's still there! Follow me!" Ellen clucked to Kona, urged him into a lope, and leaned into the gait.

Looking for all the world like a cowgirl, Darby thought. *My mother!*

"I can't ride that fast in the fog," Darby yelled.

Navigator brought her close enough to see Kona's tail fly around a turn, and Darby thought of Tutu. Hadn't they met on this path? Hadn't Tutu told her not to turn this way because it led to the old *dangerous* sugar mill?

But maybe she was wrong. One forest path looked a lot like another, she thought as her mom slowed Kona, not in a single jerk, but gradually.

Ellen's hair curled in windblown disarray against her red cheeks. She looked younger than ever before.

"What was that sound?" Darby asked as they jogged side by side. "Are you sure this is a safe place to ride?"

"I know exactly where we are and what that was," Ellen said. She drew rein, ducked her head, and pointed through a gap in the greenery.

"It looks like—bricks? Some kind of brick tower?"

"A chimney. The ruins of one, really, left over from the sugar mill. I always wanted to climb it when . . . Can you believe your mother started a thing called the

Explorers Club? We dared each other to do so many dangerous things."

If Darby's mom hadn't looked so dreamy-eyed over her childhood, she probably would have heard what she was saying. She'd accused Jonah—more than once, and in both the past and present—of keeping her too close, not letting her do anything, but clearly she'd done a lot anyway.

"Careful, there are old train tracks around here somewhere," Ellen said as Navigator followed Kona. "Past this flume, I think. Your horse can jump right over it."

Kona leaned his head to one side, as if trying to read the faded, stenciled letters on the empty flume.

"A-Z Sugar," Darby read aloud.

Kona sidestepped, rolled his eyes, and bent almost in half as Ellen urged him on. When he planted his hooves and refused, her mom did what Darby had done with Hoku just the other day: Shortening one rein, she clucked to Kona and made him turn in circles.

"Let's see if you like this," Ellen said. It was weird, because until yesterday, Darby knew she would have laughed.

Now it just looked to her as if her mom wasn't giving Kona a chance to do the right thing. When he snorted, her mother evened her reins and Kona made a clumsy high step over the empty flume.

I have to learn that bronc stop, Darby thought, but

right now she had her hands full with Navigator.

The gelding loved to jump. Though he didn't have room for a running start, he settled for a trot, then blasted off with such energy, he cleared the flume by the length of his own body.

Darby had held on tight enough to keep from falling, and her mom gave her a high five as she trotted past, trying to persuade Navigator that a walk was fast enough.

"Now, we're going to—okay, I remember. We'll pass this weird tree we used to call the witch tree. It has this long, pale root that points out in front, and another root that looks like a snake."

Roots on top of the ground? Darby was skeptical, but only for a few seconds.

"I see it," Darby said.

She also saw four stairs, probably made of stone, but it was hard to tell because they'd been blackened, maybe by a fire. The stairs climbed and stopped. Right there, along the third step, a root lay like a lounging snake.

"What are those steps for?" Darby asked.

"I don't know. Maybe part of the factory, or the plantation. There used to be houses here, too."

Darby nodded, remembering Tutu had said her cottage had been a worker's shack. Darby was about to tell her mom, but Kona was spooked by the witch tree.

He squealed and shied, then bounced off the

ground, giving a few cranky crow hops.

As bucking went, it wasn't rodeo-quality, but that was her mom in the saddle!

"Ride 'em," Darby cheered.

Giggling like a girl, Ellen managed to sound humble when she said, "I've still got it!"

Darby applauded, then dismounted along with her mother.

Once she was on the ground beside Kona, Ellen circled the gray's sweaty neck with her arms.

"I hugged Jonah's horse," she whispered to Darby. "Shhh."

"You don't have to be quiet," a voice piped up from the forest of ferns. "There's no one here but us."

Chapter Ten

Menehune.

Astonishment flashed through Darby. *Menehune* were early Hawaiians driven into hiding by tall warriors. Or helpful little people, finishing work by moonlight. Or imps.

In Darby's mind, they looked like Shakespearean fairy folk. Was she about to discover the truth?

"Aloha," Ellen called out. She looked at Darby with raised eyebrows. "Who's there?"

Her mom's voice was playful. The ride had transformed her into a carefree woman, excited rather than unnerved by the voice.

"Aloha, over here."

This time the voice was definitely human, a boy's.

As Darby and Ellen followed it, they came upon a trackside wooden dock. Legs dangling over the edge, Patrick Zink sat on the dock.

"Patrick, right?" Darby called up to him.

"Yeah, Darby and Ellen Kealoha Carter." He bowed his head, which was topped with a pith helmet. "Welcome to the A-Z Sugar Plantation. I'm one of the Z's."

Patrick appeared smaller than he had when he'd been all dressed up at Sugar Sands Cove Resort. Now his shorts showed skinned knees, and his hat—which looked like straw woven over a hard, ventilated helmet—dwarfed his freckled face.

"One of the Z's." Ellen glanced at the faded letters on the flume.

"Patrick Zink," he announced, "at your service."

Pushing his palms on the wooden dock—which was about six feet high, Darby guessed—he launched himself to the ground in front of them. The jump was meant to look like casual gallantry, but one of his ankles twisted when his hiking boots hit the ground. He fell on the seat of his khaki shorts.

Ellen's arm barred Darby from going to help him.

Patrick stood, brushed off dust, picked a sliver from his palm, then squared his hat on his head and began talking as if nothing had happened.

"I'm glad you got here before the mosquitoes came out," he said.

Darby had heard some people attracted mosquitoes

more than others. She was generally one of them, but she didn't remember seeing any in the rain forest.

"This was a sugar plantation village from about 1890 until 1950. A-Z stood for Acosta and Zink—"

"Really?" Darby gasped. "How cool!" But then her mental picture of a plantation shifted from soaring white columns to slavery. "But, 1890"—she sorted through the history notes in her brain—"there weren't slaves here, were there?"

"Hawaii wasn't exactly part of the U.S. then," her mom reminded her. "I don't think it was even a territory until about 1900." Ellen frowned as if she should remember exactly, but Darby was impressed she knew that much.

"No slaves," Patrick said, lifting a Band-Aid on his wrist, then sticking it down again. "The Acostas had a history of using them, but my dad's family voted for hiring sugar workers from Japan—like my mother's ancestors—and China, Puerto Rico, the Philippines. . . ."

"That's so interesting," Darby said.

"Hard on the land," Ellen said grimly.

Ellen's tone reminded Darby of Megan's, when she'd said Darby couldn't imagine what Cade was "capable of." It sounded like sugar farming was a crime. Or maybe it was the system her mom was thinking about, with a few rich owners who watched poorly paid people do all the work.

"Probably no worse than cattle ranching?" Darby

suggested. Something about Patrick made her want to stand up for him. Gosh, that Band-Aid didn't cover half the red swelling on his arm. "What happened to your arm?"

"Centipede," Patrick said.

"Aren't their stings poisonous?" Darby said.

"Bite," Patrick corrected. "They use their mandibles." He shifted his jaw back and forth, reminding her what a mandible was. "But it's not toxic. Unless you're allergic, and I don't think I am." He looked upward, scanning the air for insects, and his helmet fell off the back of his head. "But why take a chance and add any mosquito anticoagulant to the mix?"

His pale, freckled skin looked even whiter in contrast to his black hair. He was accident prone. His ancestors had been both overseers and laborers. And he had a killer vocabulary. Darby was wondering about Patrick's school life when he doubled back to her remark about cattle ranchers.

"Cattle ranchers and sugar plantation owners both burned off the land, so the trees wouldn't get in their way. They bought up taro land, too, and that was a native crop. But A-Z redirected the water to our fields and drained the Shining Stallion waterfall," Patrick said.

"Drained it?" Darby asked, thinking of the rainbow-spangled torrent that had hidden Black Lava's cave.

"Ran it dry," Patrick admitted.

"But that was before your time," Ellen said in a sympathetic tone.

"Yeah, but it was pretty bad. And most people remember," Patrick said. "That's why my parents are letting the forest go back to the way it was."

Darby looked around and decided the Zinks were doing a pretty good job. Except for the train tracks, the stone steps leading nowhere, the chimney jutting up from a grove of trees, and a few weathered wooden structures like the dock, most everything that was man-made was covered with vines, crowded by trees, and sprouting vegetation from age-old cracks.

Darby felt a pulse of admiration for the Zinks. If this plantation sat in Los Angeles County, the owners would have ignored their consciences and sold the land for houses, malls, and freeway on-ramps.

Navigator's whinny broke off the conversation. Especially when he was answered.

"The paint!" Ellen said, pointing.

The black-and-white horse dropped a vine from her mouth and pushed her way through a wild mass of plants that were bright green with pink flowers.

"Hey, girl," Patrick said.

"Is she your horse? She's lovely," Ellen said.

"She came from your ranch," Patrick pointed out.

"No," Darby's mom said, "she couldn't have."

But Darby imagined the horse without her black-and-white coat. Her conformation could be that of a Quarter Horse. Her tail was a little lower set than most

'Iolani Ranch horses and her hooves were broader, but even with Jonah's strict bloodlines, horses had individual differences.

"What's her name?" Darby asked.

"I gave her a new one," Patrick said, squaring his hat back in place on his head. "The name she had when my dad bought her was ugly—Mofongo."

The filly blew through her lips and shook her mane.

"I don't know what that means," Ellen said, "but it doesn't suit her."

"Is Carlos still on the ranch?" Patrick asked.

Darby shook her head.

"He's the one who named her Mofongo. It's a kind of Puerto Rican food, made with plantains and other stuff all smashed together. She was too flashy for Jonah, and he couldn't register her because of her color. So when she reached two years old and still hadn't turned bay like Luna or black like Raven—"

"Raven?" Ellen interrupted.

"That's her mom," Patrick explained. "Jonah said he'd give my dad a good deal if we took both of them. My parents aren't into horses, but I promised I'd take care of them both."

"Mofongo, out of Raven, out of Ebony," Ellen said. Smiling, she recited the filly's maternal bloodlines to Darby.

Raven's sire was no mystery now, Darby thought. The paint stallion's mark hadn't shown on Ebony's foal, Raven. But his black-and-white coloring had skipped a generation and reappeared on the wild stallion's grand-filly.

All at once Darby's heart jumped in excitement as she pictured Hoku and this pretty paint picking their way through the woods together.

"Do you ride — Mofon . . . ?" Darby tried to ask.

"I call her Mistwalker," Patrick said.

"So, that's her barn name," Ellen said.

"I guess, except, since she got loose, she's not in a barn. I don't keep her cooped up."

"How long ago did she get loose?" Darby asked.

"About a year ago."

Ellen sucked in a worried breath. "She'd be a lot safer cooped up," she said.

"Mostly she follows me around and I never go near any roads. I used to worry about her wandering off, but then she'd just come walking out of the fog, chewing a piece of *maile pilau*. And she stays on our land."

"I'm sorry to tell you this," Darby said haltingly, "but she doesn't."

"No?" Patrick asked. Mistwalker had stepped up behind him. He raised a hand to touch her face.

Darby shook her head. "She was in the fold, on 'Iolani Ranch yesterday. . . ."

Patrick turned his chin to look at the equine face beside his. "Well, still . . ."

"*And* I saw her up at Two Sisters, running with Black Lava's herd, just before the eruption."

Mistwalker nibbled Patrick's shirt collar and gave it a gentle tug, as if telling him not to believe Darby, but he did.

"You ruffian," Patrick said to his horse. Then, like an indulgent father, he changed the subject. Looking at Ellen, Patrick said, "You can ride her if you want."

"Jonah trained her?" Darby's mom asked.

Patrick nodded. "He said she was saddle broken but sassy. He's right. She lets me ride her when she feels like it and that's most of the time. At first my parents didn't want her out here with me, because they thought she was eating the native vegetation they're bringing back. But that stink vine isn't native and she loves it. So, until they can get the leaf-eating beetles from Nepal that they want to use on this stuff, they're happy to have her eat it."

Why hadn't Darby met Patrick before now? Jonah knew him. So did Megan. What about Ann? She was still sort of new to the island herself, but Darby guessed the two would get along.

"You go to Lehua High, don't you?" Darby asked.

"Sure, I've seen you there."

"What grade are you in?"

"Technically eighth, but I take some tenth-grade classes, too," he said.

Had Patrick Zink read even more books than she had? *Bet on it,* Darby thought. And he wasn't ashamed to be smart.

The thought pleased Darby until she caught her

mom looking between the two of them, smirking.

No googly eyes, Darby wanted to tell her mother, but that would have been embarrassing for all three of them.

So Darby just held her reins, leaned back against Navigator's solid shoulder, and said, "Mom, I don't have room for anything else in my life but horses."

"That's how I feel about exploring!" Patrick told her. "You're going to hear that I'm accident prone —"

Darby didn't admit she'd already heard. Instead, she blurted, "All I've heard about is your barbed-wire fences."

"Really?" Patrick said it in a contemplative way, as if he'd never thought of their fences. Then he nodded, as if making a mental note, before he continued. "It's not that I'm accident prone; it's just that I *do* stuff. I love exploring. The last time I had a cast, I was lucky —"

Darby doubted many people had ever started a sentence that way.

"—it was on my left arm. I wrote on it, *I was born for this*." He closed his eyes, savoring the words, until Mistwalker nudged him.

Patrick's exploration fever was infectious. The vine-draped steps and structures tempted Darby to learn their secrets.

"My mom used to be in an explorers club," Darby told Patrick.

When Patrick stared at her, wide-eyed, Ellen made

a "settle-down" motion with her hands. "We were little kids, Darby."

"Who else was in it?"

"No one you know," Ellen insisted.

"That's pretty implausible, Mrs. Carter. On this island, everyone knows everyone. Between the members of the Zink, Kealoha, and Kato clans, one of us knows someone from your club who's still around."

"Well." Ellen put her hands on her hips and said, "If they're responsible adults, they won't talk about it."

"And that means you won't," Darby confirmed.

"Right," her mom said, but she looked past Darby at Patrick. He rubbed his hands together, as if anticipating a great meal. "Forget it."

"Later, then," Patrick said. He looked from Darby to his horse. "I usually climb onto her back from the platform." He pointed to the thing Darby had been thinking of as a dock. "But it really is getting late. I'll saddle and bridle her and maybe you can give me a boost up?"

"Sure," Darby said, but she was watching her mother and the paint mare.

Mistwalker nuzzled Ellen's hands until she rubbed behind the horse's silvery ears.

Darby knew just what she should do with the reward money she'd received for returning Stormbird. She should buy Mistwalker for her mother. She'd only phoned Ellen for Mother's Day, and that wasn't much of a gift. Wow, not only would the mare be a dream come true for her mother, but Mistwalker belonged in Hawaii, not Pacific Pinnacles, so Ellen would have to agree that she, Darby, and their horses belonged together on Wild Horse Island.

The mare disrupted Darby's fantasy with a loud sigh. Okay, so Patrick probably wouldn't give her up. Still, it would be cool if Mom had a paint horse of her own.

"You sound like an old dog in the sun," Ellen teased. She kept petting Mistwalker as she watched Patrick jog toward a ruined building. "That holds a big grinding wheel, if no one's hauled it out." As Patrick slipped into the structure, Ellen shook her head. "He's not safe in there."

When Patrick returned with a snaffle-bitted bridle and small saddle, Mistwalker backed away from Ellen and positioned herself in front of Patrick.

"That thing looks like it's ready to fall down." Ellen nodded at the old building. "I'm surprised it hasn't been flattened by an earthquake or blown over in a storm."

She wasn't scolding him, just reminding him to be careful.

"I listen, when I'm in there. And my parents don't care."

Ellen uttered a sound of disbelief.

"Really," Patrick insisted. "My dad's into fishing, mostly, and my mom's writing a book about the plantation. As long as I keep my grades up, they don't care what I do. They say I'm a pretty low-maintenance kid, except for the doctor bills."

Patrick scratched his arms through his long sleeves. Did he have some kind of rash, or were the mosquitoes out and biting?

"What kind of saddle is that?" Darby asked.

"An endurance saddle. My mom picked it because it looked like a cross between an English-style saddle and a Western one," he said. "Mom didn't know which I wanted, but she figured she'd be at least half-right."

Mistwalker opened her mouth for the bit and rubbed her head against Patrick's chest after he'd folded her ears into the bridle's headstall. He dropped the reins and she stood waiting while Patrick tossed the saddle—made of nylon canvas instead of leather— onto her back.

"You two are quite the team," Ellen said.

"She's my best friend," Patrick said. "But I can tell she likes you. It's good for her to know other people. It really would be okay if you rode her."

"I'll remember that," Darby's mom told him.

The indulgent way she said it made Darby worry. Her mom didn't sound like she planned to spend much time hanging around the forest, where Mistwalker would appear out of the fog.

Darby handed Navigator's reins to her mom. Interlacing her fingers, she stood facing Mistwalker's tail, with her shoulder near the filly's.

Patrick was heavier than he looked, and Darby grunted with the effort needed to boost him into the saddle.

"Thanks." He settled into the small saddle, then pulled a veil-like thing down from his pith helmet. "Mosquito netting," he explained, and then waved. "See you at school!"

Listening to the filly's hoofbeats as she watched Patrick go, Darby said, "That is not an ordinary kid."

"Hawaii has its share of interesting personalities," Ellen said.

Then, as Darby started to mount up, her mother stopped her.

When she spoke, her voice sounded rehearsed. "Darby, take your boot out of the stirrup. I have to tell you something."

Chapter Eleven

"What do you have to tell me?" Darby asked.

She didn't like the sound of this.

Her mom wouldn't answer until Darby lowered herself back to the ground. She twisted the ends of her reins as she studied her mom's face.

"It's not bad," her mom insisted. "In fact, what was that expression you and Heather used to use? Oh, I know. It's a VGT."

VGT meant Very Good Thing, and her mom looked lighthearted.

But Darby's jaw tightened. She couldn't help it.

Ignoring the reins they held, Ellen took both of Darby's hands in hers, then asked, "Are you hyper-ventilating?"

"Maybe," Darby admitted.

"Stop. Here's my news: We're not poor anymore."

Not poor. When had they been poor? Didn't all mothers spend phone time talking to the bank, landlord, and power company? And the Stormbird reward was for college, so Mom must have gotten another acting job.

"This isn't a riddle, Darby. I'll tell you what I'm talking about if you'll listen."

"Okay," Darby said, but she still watched her mom's eyes, wanting to know before she was told.

"Starting in August, I'll be spending half the year in Tahiti."

"Tahiti," Darby echoed. That was where Ellen's job was now.

"While the movie shoot was delayed by rain, the early footage was making the rounds in Hollywood and it was a hit. It's gone from being a made-for-TV movie to a pilot for a new series. The producer loves the Tahitian light, color, tax advantages—and the cast."

"Especially you," Darby said.

"*Including* me."

But Ellen was being modest. Darby knew her mother would end up being the star. And a TV series meant a steady job, at least for a while.

"Since it's being shot in Tahiti, you'll be nearby." Darby tried not to celebrate too soon, but her blood was carbonated with excitement.

"Fifty-fifty," her mom said, releasing Darby's hands. "Part of it will still be shot in the Hollywood studio, so we could keep our place back home, or—"

"We're going to live in Hawaii!"

"I didn't say that," Ellen cautioned.

Darby forced herself to think past her exhilaration. She'd read that the secret to a convincing argument was slow delivery. You had to allow three seconds between each point you made. Three points, she remembered. And, you should use a low-pitched voice.

"I love my new school," she said.

One, two, three.

"I'm healthier in Hawaii," Darby pointed out.

One, two, three.

"I love Hoku and learning about horses."

Darby took a deep breath. Slow and low was working. Her mom hadn't interrupted yet.

So, why did she have to remember what Jonah had said at lunch?

"Mom, you know why else I have to stay, don't you? How many people get apprenticed to a real-live horse charmer who's training her to take over his ranch? That just doesn't happen in real life! Except for Cade, of course, but—"

Ellen pointed a resolute finger at her, and said, "Remember that, Darby. It just doesn't happen." She stopped to let her words soak in. "The very idea that he'd turn the ranch over to you is absurd."

What had gone so wrong that her mother really believed her father wouldn't leave the ranch to her, his only grandchild? This had to be about something more than Jonah not letting Ellen stay after school for play practice.

Darby tried to recall all that Jonah had said at lunch, word for word.

Not next week, you know. But, eventually, Jonah had said. Didn't her mom remember that?

"I think he meant later, when, you know . . ." Darby tried to speak slow and low, but the word *absurd* kept poking at her. "Who's going to inherit it, then? Aunt Babe? Why *not* me?"

Navigator snorted and jerked his head high against the reins. Darby wondered if she'd been shouting. Probably, because her mother waited until she'd run out of words, then changed the subject.

"Here's my plan," Ellen said. "I know you have chores, but there are—what? Two or three cowboys on that ranch."

"Three," Darby said. "But they do lots more than I do. Besides taking care of horses, they work the cattle, check the water troughs, tend sick animals, act like mechanics and plumbers. . . ."

Her mom didn't seem to have heard anything but the number.

"That's three more than there were when I lived at 'Iolani Ranch, so Jonah can do without you for a couple days while you stay with me at Aunt Babe's."

Ellen left no wiggle room in that sentence, and she wore an "or else" expression, as if she expected Darby to refuse the chance to spend time with her!

With raised eyebrows, she waited, and even though Darby would've liked it better if her mother had stayed at the ranch, getting to know Jonah again, she knew that scheme might backfire. She loved both Mom and Jonah, but right now they were a volatile combination.

"That would be so much fun, Mom!" Darby said, and she meant it. She wasn't being selfish, either. She could get her mom to say yes about staying in Hawaii just as easily at Sugar Sands Cove Resort as she could on 'Iolani Ranch. Maybe easier, without Jonah as a distraction.

Later, she'd work on bringing father and daughter back together.

Ellen's eyes sparkled and she laughed with delight. She squeezed Darby with one arm just as a niggling worry popped into Darby's mind.

"Hoku still hates men, so I'll have to see if Megan or Aunty Cathy can take care of her."

"Is there any doubt in your mind they'll do it?" her mom said against Darby's ponytail. "They're both wonderful, kind people. I can see that Megan would do anything for you, and Cathy would do anything for Jonah."

That was kind of a weird way to put it, but Darby let her mom's words lie.

* * *

Leaving 'Iolani Ranch was entirely too easy.

Jonah wasn't in sight. Cade took their horses and insisted on cooling them out and putting away their tack. Hoku wouldn't come to the fence to say good-bye.

While Darby packed an overnight bag, Ellen talked to Aunty Cathy, and Megan offered to take over Darby's chores and care for Hoku.

Megan leaned against the door frame of Darby's room. Darby sat in the middle of her bed, deciding which book to take along.

"This is only for a couple days, yeah?" Megan asked.

"Only *one*, if I can swing it," Darby whispered.

"You're crazy," Megan told her. "If I could stay at Sugar Sands, all expenses paid —"

"Do you want to come?" Darby asked. Excitement pulled her up onto her knees. "That would make it —"

"Quiet," Megan shushed her. "Really, this is one time I'm so much more mature than you. I just don't get it."

Megan's words rankled, but Darby knew she was right. There was a bigger difference between eighth and tenth grades than she'd thought — on handling parents, at least.

She sat back down, arms wrapped around her legs, and waited for Megan to tell her what to do.

"You want your mom to let you stay here, yeah?"

"Yeah."

"Go with her for as long as she wants—"

"But what about school?"

"If you think she'd really take you out of school for a vacation, she's cooler than I thought," Megan joked.

"I guess she wouldn't."

"When she's not waiting for Jonah to"—Megan gestured vaguely outside—"act like he does, and when she relaxes a little, she might see that this— that *here*—is what's best for you." Megan swallowed hard enough that Darby heard her, then looked away.

Touched by her friend's emotion, Darby was starting to go hug her when Megan held out a hand, and said, "Don't even."

Darby laughed, then realized she hadn't told Megan about her mom's news.

"Wait, I have to tell you about the TV show!"

"What TV show?"

"Swear you won't tell?"

Megan crossed her heart, and that was all the encouragement it took for Darby to repeat what her mother had told her.

Megan's eyes widened with each new detail.

"Oh my gosh. That is so cool!"

"And it's shot half on Tahiti and half in Hollywood, so it only makes sense . . ."

"What's it called?"

"*Birthright*, I think. Mom doesn't like it, but it's just a working title, and better than the first one, which was *Tahitian Sunrise* or something. She said it sounded like the name of fingernail polish."

"Oh my gosh," Megan repeated.

"Darby?" her mom called down the hallway.

"I'm almost ready," Darby said. She zipped her bag, jumped off the bed, and this time she did hug Megan. "*Mahalo*, Sis."

Darby almost made it to her mother's watermelon-colored rental car without crying.

But Jonah rode Biscuit up from the lower pastures, galloped him down the driveway, and pulled him to a stop.

Darby glanced around, sure she'd missed some emergency. There was no smoke, no earthquake-shaken buildings. No runaway horses, cows, or goats.

Jonah seemed to have galloped up here just to say good-bye.

Darby dropped her suitcase at the car and hurried toward him, but her mom, out of riding clothes and back in her dress, leaned against the car with her arms crossed, watching.

Smelling of leather and horse sweat, her grandfather caught her in a hug.

"When you come home we'll work on that bronc

stop, yeah? Don't want your little Hoku more confused than she has to be."

"It's only for a day. Or two." Darby gulped.

"I know that," he said. Setting her away from him, Jonah looked at the winged heart necklace that Darby still wore.

She tried to think of Jonah pounding the table and yelling at Mom. She tried to be angry because he'd called her a timid mouse. Nothing stopped the tears from gathering in her eyes, or her hand from closing over the gold heart charm.

Because she couldn't talk without crying, Darby flashed him a Shaka sign and headed back to the car.

"He's making me the bad guy," her mom muttered.

"Ellen!" Jonah had heard, too.

She stopped with the car door half-open.

Jonah strode closer. "I don't want to make you anything but happy. You just won't allow it."

Ellen was facing away from her, but Darby saw her mother's hand tremble, then grab onto the car door, holding herself back from another fight.

"See you later," her mom said lightly, but she slammed the car door.

My heart hurts, Darby thought. She hadn't felt like this since she was five years old, during her parents' divorce. She tried not to cry.

Ellen revved the car's engine. Darby didn't know if she did it on purpose, or because she was unfamiliar with starting it.

Either way, the sound wasn't loud enough to block out Jonah's voice. Darby wished it had been. As she looked out the car's back window, she saw him kick at the dirt. And then she heard her grandfather swear.

Chapter Twelve

It didn't make sense.

Darby didn't know why her mother and Jonah were still fighting. Obviously she hadn't read enough of her mom's diary to know what had started this feud.

Darby stared out the car window. Her chances of staying in Hawaii would improve a lot if her mom and Jonah got along.

Jonah had made his teenage daughter stay home and do chores. Darby tried to see it from his side. He was working a five-thousand-acre ranch alone. He'd just lost his wife. He needed the help and probably wanted company. A school play must have seemed pretty trivial by comparison.

Darby crossed her arms and closed her eyes, pretending to be her teenage mom. Ellen was good at acting. The school paper and her teachers had agreed on that. So she'd resented being kept away from it.

But would she leave home over it? Hold it against Jonah for over a decade?

No way.

Unless—Darby sat up straighter and opened her eyes—it had been her dream. *What if Hoku, the horse of my heart, was just a few miles away and I wasn't allowed to be with her? What if I had to stay home and wash dishes and mow lawns instead of riding? What if every day my dream dangled just out of reach?*

That would make me hold a grudge, Darby thought.

"Do you want to go back?" her mom asked.

They were stopped at the highway. Once they crossed it, they'd be at Sugar Sands Cove Resort.

"No, I want to hang out with you," Darby said.

Her mom exhaled and her shoulders sank a few inches as she said, "We'll have fun, you know. Babe's given us a suite and promised us the run of the place, for free!" She pretended to adjust her sunglasses. "This celebrity stuff might just pay off. What do you want for dinner, Hotshot?"

When Darby was a little girl learning to rollerskate, her father had called her Hotshot. He still called her by the nickname sometimes, but hearing it from her mom was a rare occasion.

Darby wound her index finger through her ponytail and hoped that the nickname was a hint that the next few days with her mother would be more than a Hawaiian slumber party.

Staying at Aunt Babe's resort was a lot different from riding on the beach next to it.

Every window had a view of the ocean, palm trees, or both.

Outside, the resort sparkled pure white, but inside it glowed with color—gold trim, bright flowers, and ceiling fans made of honey-colored wood.

Darby spotted a small sign pointing guests toward the Cultural Corner and wondered if it was like a little Hawaiian museum. She wanted to investigate, but she agreed to do it later.

Since Aunt Babe wasn't around, Darby and her mother told the front desk they'd find their suite on their own, even if it was the one farthest from the front desk.

It took a while.

"Is it still Saturday?" her mom asked, stifling a yawn when they were still searching for their suite twenty minutes later.

"I think so," Darby said. She had no idea why she'd left her riding boots on, but she was ready to take them off.

She shot a sidelong glance at her mother. Although she was still smiling, her mom had to be tired. On her "day off" she'd taken a plane at dawn, arrived at the award reception in time to impress Aunt Babe's guests, fought with her father, ridden a bucking horse—and now this.

"How many gardens does this place have?" Ellen moaned, tilting the map they'd been given.

Darby laughed. They'd crossed a shady meditation garden, a sunny massage garden, a brass sculpture garden, even a rake-the-sand garden studded with black rocks.

When they finally found their room, they didn't want to leave it, even for dinner.

Darby had never been in a place like this. Carrying her boots, she let her toes sink into a carpet that looked like a golden beach, then stood on the lanai overlooking the ocean.

When she spotted the lava-rock shower with a big window open to the sea and sky, she claimed it and left her mother to call for room service.

Lifting her arms to shampoo her hair reminded Darby of the yank against the lead rope she'd wrapped around her hand. She let warm water knead muscles that ached from her palm to her shoulder.

"I ordered a pizza sampler," her mom said as Darby appeared with a towel wrapped around her wet hair. "A bunch of mini pizzas—all your favorites, plus goat cheese and porcini mushrooms for me."

Ellen made a whirlwind trip to the shower next, and even before the pizza arrived she and Darby began catching up on what they'd missed while being apart. Both sat cross-legged on their beds as Darby described a typical day on 'Iolani Ranch.

Darby told her mother about her chores, her new favorite foods, and when Ellen asked about her new friends, Darby described people she talked to in each of her classes and, of course, Ann.

"Ann sounds great," Ellen said. "What does Jonah think of her?"

"He calls her Wild Ann," Darby began.

"*Jonah* calls her wild?" her mother asked with a quick intake of breath.

Reflexively Darby's spine straightened, and her mother must have noticed.

"Ann's the red-haired girl you introduced me to, right? From Nevada." She waited for Darby to nod. "I'm eager to get to know her better." Ellen made a gesture that seemed to brush away her worries. "And Megan?"

Darby explained that she and Megan were the best of friends, too, and even confided the misunderstanding that had lasted between Megan and Cade for years.

"Tutu told me I was a natural at conducting *ho'oponopono* when she found out I got them talking." Darby stumbled over the Hawaiian term that meant an ancient problem-solving process, kind of like something a counselor would use, but she still felt proud.

Answering the soft knock at the door, her mother

smiled over her shoulder and said, "Let me give you a tip: Don't try practicing your *ho'oponopono* skills on me."

The aroma of oregano and cheese puffed into the room as Ellen removed a silver dome from the tray of treats, and Darby could only listen and eat as her mother told her about her working life in Tahiti.

"I've never spent so much time with the same cast and crew," her mother said. She sipped her diet cola thoughtfully. "At the risk of sounding sappy, I have to tell you, it really is like a big family."

Just as her mother had bitten back her views on Ann, Darby didn't point out that her mother already had a great family she should get to know better.

"What about your cousin Duxelles?" Ellen asked suddenly.

Darby groaned.

"She's a striking girl, but she looks unhappy," Ellen said.

"Funny you should use the word *striking*." Darby didn't choke back her sarcasm, but she did explain that her cousin's bullying didn't stop short of shoves and stinging finger flicks. "The nicest thing I can say about her is she's a strong swimmer. The one time I actually liked Duckie—"

"Duckie?"

"—was when she helped rescue the foals from the churned-up water after the tsunami."

Ellen's eyes widened, grew angry, then worried, and finally shone with laughter as Darby explained how Duckie had gotten her nickname.

Satisfied and drowsy with dinner and gossip, Darby turned down her mother's offer of watching an in-room movie.

"Maybe tomorrow night," Ellen said. She tucked Darby into bed as if she were a child, but Darby didn't protest.

Sometime her mother slipped into the bed next to her. Sometime she turned out the bedside lamp. And sometime, just before her eyes closed for the night, Darby said, "I loved watching you ride, Mama," but she was asleep before Ellen answered.

The next day, Darby's mother and Aunt Babe taught her what it meant to be pampered.

For breakfast, she ate taro and mango pancakes with toasted coconut sprinkles. Next, she snorkeled in a pool surrounded by lava rocks and filled with native fish. After that, her mother let her drive a golf cart on their spin around the resort grounds.

Lunch was ti leaf–wrapped fish. It was delicious, but a little weird. She didn't know if she was supposed to eat the ti leaf, and the fish looked just like one she'd swum next to an hour before.

The hotel's Cultural Corner turned out to be a gift shop. It had a wall of portraits and replicas of artifacts that reminded her of the ancient necklace that had attached itself to her on the pali, but when her mom offered to buy her a souvenir, Darby didn't see anything she wanted. She didn't need a trinket to keep her smiling, because Ellen looked more content every moment, and that made Darby happy, too.

When they were having an afternoon snack of passion fruit, pineapple, and papaya ice cream with lavender sauce at an outside table, Ellen lowered the sunglasses covering her eyes and looked at Darby.

"If we did stay, you'd have to attend a private school," Ellen said, "and that takes a lot of money."

Darby sat back in her chair. Her impulse was to bounce around crowing with delight, but she thought of Megan's advice to hang back.

Taking a deep breath, Darby said, "I wouldn't have to. I like my school."

"The public schools here aren't that good, honey. Everyone knows that."

"But wait, the Potters—you know, Ann's family—well, not to be impolite, but her family has tons of money and Ann goes to Lehua High School. And Mom, *you* went to Lehua! What better endorsement could they get than that?"

"Come on, sweet talker," her mom said, pushing her sunglasses back into position. Then she stood and adjusted her straw hat to protect her complexion. "Let's change into dry swimsuits and go back to the beach."

The next morning, Ellen let Darby oversleep on purpose and called her school to say Darby was out on family business.

Is this bribery? Darby wanted to ask, but instead she raced her mom up the resort's climbing wall, wearing the cute little skirt Aunt Babe had given her to play tennis in—which she did badly—and swam some more before lunch.

It wasn't until Flight's neigh stopped Darby from chewing a macadamia-crusted prawn and she stared into the air, thinking of Hoku, that Ellen said, "You're not enjoying this, are you?"

"Are you kidding? Of course I am!" Darby said, and she meant it.

Why would Ellen say such a thing?

"But you'd rather be with your horse than your mother."

"No. No way." Darby shook her head so hard, her wet ponytail slapped her cheeks.

"Go ahead, honey, be honest."

"Mom, don't you think you're being kind of paranoid?" Darby asked, but Ellen just sat back, studying her, waiting for her daughter to give the question more thought. "Okay. It's true that if I had to choose between 'Iolani Ranch's green grass and that golf course for the rest of my life, I'd pick the ranch. And if I had to pick Sugar Sands' lava lagoon or the ocean, I'd pick the ocean. But this is totally fun, like a vacation."

Darby didn't flinch away, but she was curious when her mother reached for her ponytail.

"This confirms it," her mother said. "See the reddish tips on your black ponytail? They're sunburnt.

You've turned into an outdoor girl."

"Of course," Darby said, thinking of her mom riding headlong into the rain forest. "It's in my blood. I was born into the Explorers Club."

"I don't know." Her mom stretched like a cat. "I could get used to this. Your aunt Babe has offered to let us live here rent free, with maid service."

Darby froze.

She thought of a mouse in the owl's shadow.

Stay still, stay very still, she told herself.

She wanted to stay in Hawaii, but not here.

"You can breathe," her mom said. "I told her we'd have to think about it."

"It's an incredible offer," Darby admitted.

"And I haven't said no."

Darby nodded. Looking at the offer from Ellen's point of view, she must be flattered that Aunt Babe wanted her here for her star power.

"I don't have to go back to work until Wednesday morning," her mom said, "but it's important you get back to school—part of this decision is going to be based on your grades, young lady . . ."

"Good," Darby said, and she meant it. The only class she'd fallen below an A in was Ecology, and Mr. Silva was acknowledged to be a real warlock when it came to makeup work. She'd better remember that.

But her mom was still talking.

". . . and Cathy said she'd like to pick you up after Megan's soccer practice today and take you back to the ranch. Hoku's making a nuisance of herself."

"Hoku? What's wrong?" Darby asked.

"She's fine, but she's neighing incessantly. For you, probably."

"Aw, poor Hoku," Darby said, and she knew how the filly felt. "But, what will you do—"

"Without you?" Ellen kissed Darby's cheek. "I'll console myself with a massage in the massage garden, maybe have breakfast in bed. . . ."

Darby smiled. After living in a bunch of low-rent apartments, working low-paying jobs while she polished her acting skills and took care of her daughter, Ellen was enjoying this taste of luxury.

"Okay," Darby said. "But before you leave, can we go ride together once more?"

And since I've been the most patient human on earth, can you tell me then whether we can stay in Hawaii?

"Absolutely. Tuesday afternoon. It's a date!" Ellen said, and then she dumped the contents of a sterling-silver sugar bowl into a cloth napkin, knotted the top, and handed it to Darby. "Until then, tell the horses I said aloha."

Megan looked longingly over her shoulder as the white hotel grew smaller out the SUV's back window. "Restaurant meals, maids, and massages? What a drag, yeah?"

"I know, it's awful of me not to appreciate it more," Darby said as Megan begged for details of her days at the resort, "but it's just not my thing."

"It's *my* thing," Megan whined.

"Megan," Aunty Cathy scolded.

"So, Hoku's sad?" Darby asked.

"Sad?" Aunty Cathy met Darby's eyes in the rearview mirror. "No, I'd say she can't believe you'd go off and leave her. What would you say, Megan?"

"Incredulity." Megan stretched the word out. "It's one of my vocabulary words in English this week. Let me use it in a sentence for you. 'Hoku is in a state of *incredulity*, because no one abandons the mustang princess.'"

"I think you're the one Darby shouldn't leave alone," Aunty Cathy said.

"I'm just excited because I don't have any chores for two days," Megan reminded Darby.

"I know." Darby groaned. But she really didn't mind.

This was real life, she thought. Teasing and chores. And if it was wrong of her not to appreciate the resort, but to feel pleased that Hoku missed her, then oh, well.

"You'll be able to hear Hoku before you see her," Aunty Cathy said, and Darby smiled as she looked out the window.

She could hardly wait.

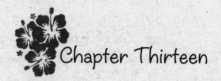

Chapter Thirteen

With Conch ground-tied nearby, getting used to the sight of dirt flying from a shovel, Kimo dug holes along the fence line with the Zinks.

"Your horse, she's pretty darn aggravated," Kimo said when he spotted Darby.

Darby heard Hoku's imperious neighs.

"Listen to her," Cade called as he walked from the ranch office toward her and Kimo. "She thinks you'd better get yourself on down to that corral right this minute."

Darby laughed and took the pink slip of paper Cade handed her. Before she could read it, Cade tapped the note.

"Call Ann Potter," he said, then squinted as if

stunned by the sound waves of Hoku's whinny. "If you're up for learning that bronc stop, now'd be a good time to try it," Cade said. "She's apt to pull something."

"Sure, I'm up for it," Darby said, trying not to imagine the shock of her bones colliding with the earth.

"Yeah, *keiki,*" Kimo said, calling her "kid," "you been gone so long, I'm, uh, you know—" He looked meaningfully at Cade.

"What?" The young paniolo definitely wasn't getting Kimo's message. Cade appeared mystified.

"You know da kine—PhD."

"PhD?" Darby asked. It was a college degree; she knew that much. But was Kimo saying he'd earned a PhD in the two days she'd been gone?

It had to be some kind of joke, and when she glanced over at Cade, his stifled smile made it clear that he'd heard this before.

"Okay," Darby said, taking the bait, "I was gone so long that you got a PhD?"

"No, I *am* a PhD," he repeated slowly. "Post-hole digger, yeah?"

Darby rolled her eyes at the joke, but Kimo chuckled to himself as Cade explained that the Zinks had called Jonah to say they'd gladly pay for a new wooden fence if 'Iolani Ranch donated the labor.

"They said they never realized the barbed wire was dangerous," Cade told her. He shook his head.

"Wonder what made 'em think of it now."

Darby knew. She remembered the thoughtful way that Patrick had taken in her remark that all she knew about him was that his family had barbed-wire fences.

But she didn't pause to discuss the Zinks with Cade and Kimo.

She was headed for her horse.

Hoku fell quiet the minute she could see and be seen. She'd only been calling, like one herd member for another who'd fallen behind or been lost, Darby thought. Now that Hoku saw her, the filly communicated silently, as any wild horse would.

Hoku's ears tipped so far forward, they almost touched her brow. Her nostrils flared wide, searching for scent clues to Darby's disappearance.

"I'm sorry, girl," Darby said softly. "If you could've understood where I was going, I would have told you."

Curiosity remained Hoku's primary mood until Darby passed the fence. Once Darby was inside the corral, the wild filly's attitude changed.

Head held high, tail upflung and streaming, Hoku circled the corral at a gallop.

Darby squinted against the dust, until the sorrel stopped and advanced. Ears pointed sideways, head tilted, and lips protruding like she was asking for a kiss, Hoku came closer.

Darby recognized the signs as playfulness, but she wondered what came next. The relaxed eyes, the lips . . .

"I don't think so!" Darby jumped aside as Hoku tried to give her a mischievous nip. "We don't have the same kind of skin, girl."

Hoku tossed her forelock from her face and pranced a circle around Darby. Though the filly's lips wore an expression equivalent to a human smile, Darby stayed on her toes, ready to dart away. Even if it was given in affection, a nip would hurt.

But Hoku had stopped playing. She sniffed, nostrils sucking in scents from Darby's ankles to her collarbone. Then she stamped, looked away, and swished her tail.

"Ready to ride?" Darby asked her horse.

Hoku yawned, but her boredom disappeared when Darby offered the halter. Hoku shoved her muzzle toward the nosepiece. Once the halter was buckled, she bumped her rump against Darby, asking why she didn't use the fence to climb on.

"I'm taking you to the round pen," she told the filly. "Then I'll get on."

Frustrated with the delay, Hoku lunged to the end of her striped rope and led the way.

Cade held the gate open.

"Do you remember what set her off last time you tried that one-rein stop?" Cade asked. His voice made Hoku flash her ears backward in a token warning, but she didn't pause to threaten him.

"Sure, it was the farrier's stupid truck backfiring and me not paying attention," Darby said. She tried to keep the irritation out of her voice as she mounted Hoku.

Once Darby had positioned herself on the filly's back, holding the lead rope rein, Hoku lowered her head, then sighed in contentment as if she'd been thrown a forkful of hay.

"I'm glad to be back," Darby whispered to her horse.

"Just ride her around the fence line, nice and easy," Cade said as he climbed the outside of the round pen, "while I tell you what me and Kit figured out.

"A horse likes to travel straight. That's how she's balanced and safe. When she's bent like you had her the other day, only one idea's poundin' through her brain. 'I gotta get straight. If I run in circles, something will eat me.'"

Darby rode Hoku around the corral at a smooth walk. Riding bareback, she felt no tension in the filly's muscles, so she listened to Cade and tried to memorize every word.

"But the rider's thinking, 'I've gotta stop her and show her I've got control.' Now, folks have been doing that with one rein for a long time, but they've also found that lots of horses keep going, and they get fallen on.

"And if you depend on that one-rein stop, what

happens on a skinny mountain trail? If Hoku scents something prowling and she's scared enough when you bend her, you're both going off the edge."

Kimo walked up to the pen, shovel over his shoulder, with the grulla gelding following.

"Tell you what else," Kimo said. "You pull her around like that too often, it gets just like weight lifting, yeah? Pretty soon Hoku's got strong muscles in her neck and she pulls *back*. Or spooks every time you jiggle a rein, afraid you're going to spin her."

Hoku picked her hooves up in a perfect cow-horse jog.

"So what do I do instead?" Darby asked. "If Pip came yapping into the corral and Hoku started acting up? And what does this have to do with 'broncs'?"

"It's real simple," Cade said. "Listen first; then you can try it, if you're real gentle."

"I always am," Darby insisted, and she felt good when Cade nodded in agreement.

"This is what you'll do: Pull one side of the rein back toward your belt buckle, not hard, now, and lift the other up toward your breastbone. It'd be easier for her to understand if you had split reins, but we'll start with what she's used to."

Darby watched Hoku's ears. They didn't flatten in irritation, just stayed where they were as she lifted her head. She slowed, but made no jerky, panicky movements.

"Good girl," Darby told her horse.

"Now here comes Jonah. How's she feel about the ATV?" Cade asked.

Darby didn't answer. Instead she read Hoku's body language. The filly's sides heated under Darby's knees. A trot lengthened into an unruly half lope as Hoku veered to the far side of the round pen.

"Now," Cade urged softly.

Darby drew one side of the rope back to her belt buckle and lifted the other toward her sternum. Hoku's front hooves lifted an inch or so off the ground before she continued to jog around the pen.

"Yes!" Cade shouted, and his yell meant Darby had to go through the maneuver again, because Hoku objected to his noise. "How simple is that! You gave her the chance to do right, and she did!"

Darby worked with her horse until dark, letting her know she was home.

"For good, I hope," she told Hoku. And when she confessed that she'd left the sugar in her suitcase, Hoku didn't mind.

Hay and Darby were enough.

Darby's legs were weak from exertion. Riding, tennis, rock climbing, and swimming had caught up with her muscles by the time she made it into Sun House. Her ankles ached as she tugged off her boots, then slumped against the wall behind the entrance hall bench.

Two days away from Hoku had seemed like forever,

but it had been nice of her mom to let her return without making her feel guilty.

Darby smiled to herself as she made it down the hall, threw her riding clothes into the hamper, showered, and then tottered into her room. She laid out school clothes for the next day—what was it? Monday? No, Tuesday—and set her alarm clock to go off a little later than usual.

It felt good to crawl into her own bed.

The phone rang. Darby's eyes popped open. Five thirty.

Darby closed her eyes and listened. Why wasn't Jonah hurrying to answer it? Could he already be up and outside? Probably.

Eyes still closed, Darby rolled out of bed and used the wall to guide herself out of her room and down the hall, until she reached the kitchen. And the phone.

"Hello?"

"You didn't call me back last night."

It was Ann.

"I'm so sorry," Darby muttered.

"Not"—Ann interrupted herself with a yawn—"as sorry as you're going to be."

Darby blinked. She opened one eye all the way and asked, "What do you mean?"

For a second they both yawned, but Ann sounded awake as she said, "You need to do an experiment off that list Mr. Silva gave us before spring break. It's due today. No excuses. He assigned people to call everyone who was absent. 'Everyone' included *you*."

Mr. Silva, the warlock of makeup work. Her only falling grade.

Mom, the ruler of her future. *Part of this decision will be based on your grades, young lady.*

"Darby? Did you go back to sleep?"

"No. Of course not. Sleeping, I could never dream up such a good friend. You woke up at dawn to call me when—"

"You can kiss my feet at school. Right now, you'd better get started. You do have that handout, right?"

"Is it on blue paper?" Darby asked.

"Yep, and let me give you a tip. Look at the list of experiments titled 'Includes only ingredients commonly found in home kitchen.'"

"Perfect." Darby's gaze shifted to the kitchen window. A soft rain hissed against the grass outside. Lots of people thought rain was good luck, but she crossed her fingers, just to be safe.

"There's a test when class starts. That's when you write up your results. Now, just do the experiment and observe. Good night."

"What do you mean? It's morning."

"Not for me," Ann said through a yawn. "I can sleep for another hour."

"I know how I'm going to repay you!" Darby yelled before Ann could hang up. "You're going to be a member of the Explorers Club."

"I'm not asking what that is. I might have trouble falling asleep."

As soon as Ann hung up, Darby retrieved her handout and skimmed the topics. Then, to remind Mr. Silva of the high grade she and Ann had gotten on their volcanic observation, Darby picked a volcano experiment.

Good old Mr. Silva, Darby thought as she searched out a large plastic soda bottle, dish-washing soap, baking soda, vinegar, and red food coloring. He really tried to make science fun.

She couldn't find a pan like the one in the picture, but she could probably do without it, since she wasn't carrying the experiment to school.

Darby tipped over the plastic bottle with her elbow. After setting it upright, she spilled the last tablespoon of baking soda she was measuring into the bottle.

Wake up, Darby ordered herself.

Darby added a pinch more baking soda to make up for what she'd spilled.

Next, she added a few squirts of detergent and a drop of food coloring, and poured in enough vinegar to cover the stuff in the bottom of the bottle.

Darby was rolling the stiffness from her shoulders and wondering how Patrick Zink's centipede bite felt, when she realized she should have read all of the directions before she started.

The baking soda and detergent had just been sitting there innocently until she'd added the vinegar. Now that the vinegar had mixed with soda, fizzing bubbles of gas forced suds up the bottle's neck.

"And this is when the pan would have been handy," Darby muttered.

The foamy mess overflowed onto the kitchen counter. And beyond. Would the bottle ever stop streaming pretend pink lava?

Darby tried to enjoy the overflowing ooze, since she couldn't look away. She had to let the experiment trash the kitchen, understand what was happening, and hope there was still time to clean up.

After all, she had to do an A-level job of documenting this on her test. She was determined to stay on 'Iolani Ranch, so she'd leave nothing to chance.

 Chapter Fourteen

Darby planned to introduce Patrick and Ann before school that day. They'd arranged to meet on the Link, a bridge that vaulted high over the center of the school, giving everyone who stood there a view of the complete campus.

"I've seen him, of course, but I've never had a class with Patrick Zink," Ann said as she and Darby headed for the Link. When Ann lowered her voice, Darby could tell she was a bit ashamed to ask, "He's . . . is he weird?"

"It depends," Darby said, shrugging. "Maybe a little, but he's got an amazing paint horse, Mistwalker. He changed her name from Mofongo—"

"That's a plus," Ann said.

"And he knows the ruins of the old sugar planta-tion like it's his personal playground, which it pretty much *is* —"

"Because his parents own it," Ann finished for her. "So, he's rich?"

"I try not to hold that against him, since my best friend is rich," Darby teased.

"No, we're not," Ann said. "Just last night my dad was saying we're right back where we were when we lived in Nevada. Land and horse rich, but money poor."

"Anyway," Darby went on, "I get the feeling he's so smart he makes both of us look like slackers."

Patrick and Ann hit it off immediately. In fact, Darby was almost late to class because of them. Darby realized the two had become instant friends when she had to leave them talking.

As she hurried to class, Darby heard Patrick's voice saying, "Actually, the centipede's bite is painful but not deadly."

Ann caught up with Darby just outside Miss Day's English classroom, and Ann agreed she wanted to go exploring with Patrick. They'd decided to meet after school and ride out to the sugar mill. Ann had never been there, and she was eager to meet Mistwalker, too.

Just before the bell rang, Ann stopped to rub the knee she'd injured playing soccer and asked, "So, all the Band-Aids and casts . . . ?"

Darby shrugged again. "To tell you the truth, I

don't know whether he's accident prone or just plain fearless, but I guess we'll find out."

Some days at school are so great, it's like your brain is Velcro, Darby thought later.

In English, Miss Day was talking about the author Madeleine L'Engle again, and she wrote her favorite L'Engle quotation on the board.

"'Love isn't what you feel, it's what you do,'" Miss Day read, and everyone must have immediately gotten it like she did, Darby thought, because they all wrote it down.

The quotation had to be banished while Darby was hunched over her Ecology test, writing up the results of this morning's experiment. She glanced up at the clock and caught Mr. Silva looking over her shoulder, reading her analysis and chuckling.

For an instant she was worried, but he gave her a thumbs-up and continued prowling the rows of desks.

P.E. was rained out, so Miss Day had the class count off by threes. The "ones" would have a "crunch" competition. The "twos" would act as spotters and record the results.

"The threes—"

Darby's eyes squinched shut. Her muscles would protest almost any task.

"—will have silent study hall in the library."

Darby's fist shot toward the ceiling, celebrating

without her consent before she calmly folded her arms together and tried to look studious.

That afternoon, Darby took special care grooming Navigator.

"You're a muddy mess," she said, then dragged a mounting block up beside the big gelding so she could reach his back.

Navigator loved mud puddles, and she had to use a rubber curry comb to loosen slabs and flakes of mud from his hair before she could even think of using a brush.

"It would have been lots easier to ride Hoku," she told him, but Darby knew that wouldn't have been a great idea.

Mistwalker was young and flighty. Patrick had said the filly allowed him to ride "when she felt like it."

Ann's horse was Sugarfoot. The gelding was beautiful, a caramel-and-white paint, and though his training was coming along, he was still a "chaser." According to Ann, the best thing to do if Sugarfoot set upon you was "stand your ground and holler."

"Not good playmates for Hoku," Darby told Navigator as she dabbed a damp sponge at the corner of his eye. "But I don't think you'll be corrupted."

Navigator stared at her. The rust-colored hair circling his eyes gave him a wise look.

You can depend on me, Navigator seemed to say, and Darby did. The seventeen-hand-high gelding had earned his name by finding his way home from every place on the island.

"You're the fastest trail guide around these parts," she drawled to him.

"Don't sweet-talk my horses," Jonah's voice pleaded, but Darby could see he was joking.

"I forgot," Darby said, although she knew he wouldn't believe her for a second.

"Off to ride with Wild Ann and the Zink boy, yeah?"

"Yep, but I'm running late," Darby said.

"Tell 'em since you're no *malihini* anymore," he said, taking the saddle from her arms, "you're runnin' on Hawaiian time."

Darby shivered with delight. Not because Jonah had relieved her of the burden, but because he'd reclassified her. In his eyes, she wasn't a newcomer anymore.

Jonah settled her saddle on the woven saddle blanket and fed the cinch through the buckle without looking.

"You the one who put him onto this fence deal?" Jonah asked.

"Patrick? Well, sort of. I just mentioned all I knew about his family was that they used barbed wire," Darby admitted.

Jonah didn't comment on whether or not that was rude. He just nodded and used his boot to move the mounting block next to Navigator.

Once Darby was in the saddle, he said, "Thought your mother was coming to ride today."

Startled, Darby tried to remember exactly what her mother had said. She remembered the discussion of private school and the napkin full of sugar cubes. But for some reason she wasn't sure if her mother had said they'd ride on Tuesday or Wednesday. Finally, she said, "Tomorrow, I think."

Jonah shrugged and turned his wrist in a Shaka.

"Have fun," he said. And then, just as she was passing Sun House, he called after her.

"Granddaughter!"

"Yes?"

"Good call not taking your filly."

"Thank—"

"Don't think she'd care much for those train tracks."

Darby rode on, smiling, until Navigator hopped over the cattle guard at the ranch's front gate. Only then did it occur to her that Jonah knew exactly where she was going.

Her smile faltered briefly until a second revelation hit her. If Jonah knew where *she* was going to explore, he'd probably known about her mom's explorations, too.

Darby heard Patrick and Ann chattering as she approached the neighbor's laundry line, where they'd agreed to meet.

"But see, when I moved here, people told me the Zinks were lazy."

Darby gasped at Ann's remark, but Patrick didn't sound like he'd taken offense.

"To a certain extent they are—not me, because I'm going to school—but my parents are both just doing their own things while they wait for the land to return to its original state. Their ancestors ruined the land, but sometimes you have to break with the ancestors and do what's right."

By the time Darby rode Navigator into sight, Ann and Patrick had progressed from Patrick's theory on ancestor reverence to Ann's wondering which undiscovered species of wildlife would have remained if the burning of the forest and realignment of traditional water courses hadn't happened.

Instead of Sugarfoot, Ann rode Soda, a blackish-blue roan, which startled at the sight of Navigator. Patrick sat with bare legs dangling astride Mistwalker.

"Don't mind me," Darby said as she halted her dark gelding near her friends.

"Aloha!" Patrick said, and Mistwalker surged forward. By nibbling his mane she reminded Navigator they'd met before.

"She looks beautiful," Darby said.

"My mom bought the bridle and I had to cut it down to fit, but it hardly shows, does it?"

"Not at all," Darby said.

The black leather headstall was a single strap polished to a high shine, attached to a silver D-ring bit.

Soda mouthed his own bit, loudly and nervously. The gelding had been kept in a stall "no bigger than a bathtub" for most of his life, according to Ann, who'd been with her parents when they rescued the horse from his neglectful owner on the island of Kauai.

"And you look pretty, too, Soda," Darby said, smooching at the horse. He looked up at her, surprised, but not scared.

Darby was about to try to pet Soda when Navigator protested the special treatment he was getting from Mistwalker.

Tired of the paint grooming him with tiny bites that had moved from his mane to his tail, Navigator gave a short squeal and swung his head in her direction.

"Hey! It's not customary to snack on your friends," Patrick scolded Mistwalker.

The mare looked back at him and blinked. Then, not a bit ashamed, she feinted a nip at the toe showing through a hole in his sneaker.

Ann and Darby laughed, especially when Mistwalker shook all over, from nose to tail, quite pleased with herself.

Still, Darby couldn't help recalling the lecture she'd received from her grandfather when she wasn't wearing riding boots.

She didn't want to sound bossy, though, since she hardly knew Patrick. So she was happy when Ann suggested, "You might want to wear boots when you ride."

Patrick looked down past his khaki shorts to his matching sneakers, then up at the girls.

"It's my understanding that boots are only safer because it's more difficult for the foot to slip through the stirrup, leaving the rider entrapped and in danger of being dragged to death," Patrick said.

"That's what Jonah told me," Darby agreed.

"I'm riding bareback," he pointed out.

While he leaned forward to pat Mistwalker's satiny neck, Ann's eyes met Darby's. Neither of them had a rebuttal for Patrick's logic, but Darby wasn't convinced. Patrick's holey canvas shoes just weren't suitable for riding, especially out in the rain forest.

Birds took wing at the sounds of their conversation as they rode deeper into the rain forest. Ann and Patrick did most of the talking, because the whole time they rode toward the old plantation, Darby thought of Tutu.

There hadn't been time for her mom to see Tutu during their first ride, and Ellen had seemed downhearted about it. But that wasn't why Darby thought of Tutu.

Her great-grandmother was a *kupuna*, a respected elder, and she'd warned Darby not to take this path toward the ruined plantation because it was dangerous.

What kind of trouble had Tutu worried about? Maybe she was just afraid of Darby getting lost, because she didn't know her way around. Patrick appeared to know every twig and trail on his family's plantation, so that shouldn't be a problem.

Still, riding out here with Mom had felt different. Ellen had been there a million times before and she'd pointed out railroad tracks and rocks and vines. Patrick and Ann were preoccupied with their new friendship and discussing complex topics.

"So, where did all the houses go?" Ann asked Patrick.

He explained his parents' goal of letting the rain forest reclaim human structures, and told her, just as he had Darby and her mother, about the cultural mix of workers in the plantation's history.

"And this is where my mom and her friends had their Explorers Club," Darby said as they rode through a row of sunbeams that had struggled through the trees.

"Hey, what are we going to do for initiation into *our* Explorers Club?" Ann asked.

For a moment, Darby thought Ann's blue eyes turned a little sly and her red hair, struck by the sun, appeared to be scattered with sparks. Patrick dropped his reins and let Mistwalker prance on without guidance, as he rubbed his palms together.

He turned his freckled face toward Ann's, clearly expecting her to lead him into some new amusement.

Wild Ann. No one at school would believe that Patrick and Ann could lead each other into mischief, Darby thought.

She noticed how the sun glazed over the lenses

of Patrick's glasses. Could he be blinded by having friends in this jungle where he was usually all alone?

Patrick threw himself off Mistwalker. The mare lowered her head. There was a clang of teeth on metal as Patrick pulled off the black leather bridle, hung it on a low branch, and made a cluck that sent the mare trotting into the forest.

Using neck ropes, Darby and Ann tethered Navigator and Soda to a length of pierced iron that neither of them could identify, while Patrick retrieved his pith helmet from the abandoned mill building.

"It's just electrifying to have partners in crime," Patrick teased as the girls faced him with their hands on their hips.

Ann's wildness was contagious to Patrick, but had the opposite effect on Darby. She hoped her uneasiness didn't have anything to do with her horse-charmer instincts, her *ho'oponopono* sensitivity, or wise-woman genes she'd inherited from her great-grandmother.

Such thoughts were just ridiculous, but what was going on? She'd climbed the pali, swum in dangerous waters, and lain in the snow with a wild horse. She was not a scaredy-cat.

Still, Darby heard herself speaking as if she were a chaperone for the other two: "It's going to be dark in an hour or so." Then she could hardly believe she added, "I'm not sure we have time for an initiation."

Ann and Patrick turned to look at her, as if she'd

spoken a different language. But their stares only lasted a second.

They returned to arguing. Patrick tried to make a case for "tightrope walking" the edge of the dock that had once served as a loading point for the narrow-gauge railroad that ran to a pier at Crescent Cove.

"That's enough of a challenge to start with," he said sensibly.

"I've got to climb that," Ann said, pointing at a brick chimney.

All three of them shaded their eyes and tilted their heads back to study the structure. About as tall as a two-story house, it soared through the trees, toward the sky.

"Nothing else will do," Ann said dreamily. "It looks like a red castle used to surround it."

"No way," Darby said. She crossed her arms, then rubbed them, thinking of mosquitoes.

You wimp, she called herself, but her mind wouldn't be talked out of its anxiety.

"I guess you're right," Ann said, then asked Patrick, "I don't suppose there's a haunted mansion? An overseer's house or something?"

"There was! Let me think where," Patrick answered.

This is like adding the vinegar, Darby thought. She frowned at Ann and thought of her science experiment. Any two of them would have been okay, but the three of them together—okay, just Ann and Patrick—

were too crazy together.

And being the sensible one was just no fun.

"How about this," Darby proposed. "We'll do Patrick's idea first, since he's familiar with the area—"

"Kind of like follow the leader!" Patrick rejoiced.

"—and then we'll climb the chimney next time we come."

"Let's hurry," Ann said, then called over her shoulder, "It's okay, boy."

Her voice did nothing to calm Soda. His hindquarters swung against Navigator's, and he pawed at the ground.

"Excess energy," Ann diagnosed, but Darby thought Soda was as worried as she was. When Ann looked back at the brick chimney, Darby decided Soda probably had better sense than his owner.

"We're agreed we can't climb that thing after sundown, right?" Darby insisted, pointing at the chimney.

"Right!" Patrick said; then he and Darby turned toward Ann.

"Okay, I give in," she said, "but I don't know why. I'll be dead if I get home after sundown anyway, so what do I have to lose?"

As they climbed the wooden structure, snaking their fingers through vines, trying to get footholds on squeaky old crossbeams, Ann started talking like a pirate.

"Patrick the pirate, argh!" Ann growled. "Watch where ye be putting yer scurvy feet or ye'll crush me fingers."

"Avast, me ladies—"

"You mean laddies," Ann corrected.

"No—"

Darby stopped listening as Patrick began explaining the derivation of the word *buccaneer*. It had something to do with barbecued goats, and that was a topic she was trying not to think about, because Jonah claimed he wanted to cook Francie on the Fourth of July.

So Darby was daydreaming.

One minute, she was waiting her turn to "walk the plank" of the old loading dock. Filling the minutes while the others walked ahead of her, she'd stared past lehua blossoms to clouds following the summit line of far-off hills.

The next minute would have been about the same if she'd known why Patrick ordered Ann to "Walk right on the edge, me hearty," but Darby was wondering if a rainstorm was brewing, and trying to tell apart the calls of one honey creeper from another.

Maybe the honey creepers' calls were a warning.

Darby heard a creak. She tried to see around Ann, but a rotten board had already cracked, and Patrick was gone. There was no time to grab for him or keep his yelp from being cut short by an awful impact.

Chapter Fifteen

The afterimage of Ann following right behind Patrick hung before Darby's stunned eyes. Ann was about an arm's length ahead of Darby. Ann wobbled a little, placing her boots where Patrick's sneakers had skimmed on ahead.

Darby didn't know why they'd been walking on the edge of the dock. Though Darby's view was mostly blocked by Ann, she'd seen Patrick's arms fly out from his sides, fighting for balance, just before the crash.

Who was screaming?

Not Ann. She stood with her hands gripping her hips. Looking down, she shivered.

"I can hear my d-dad now," Ann tried to joke, so Patrick couldn't have fallen off the edge. "If you k-kids hadn't been—if—"

Patrick's groan didn't sound human.

Darby cut around Ann. It took her a minute to make sense of everything.

At first, Darby had the ludicrous impression that Patrick was squatting like a laying hen. Except that Patrick's right leg had disappeared from sight. It vanished into a splintered hole in the dock. He'd kept himself from falling the rest of the way through by bracing his hands on each side of the snug opening. His other leg was kinked up at a tight angle against his chest, and though his ripped sneaker was flat, his torso swayed as if he couldn't hold himself up much longer.

"I'm gonna fall."

"No, you're not," Darby said. She squatted next to him.

Ann managed to make her way around them both. Then she slipped her hands under Patrick's arms.

Darby realized the screams were coming from Mistwalker. The black-and-white mare paced below them, neighing.

"Don't pull me up!" Patrick howled. "I'm caught. There's wood in my leg! It stabbed into my thigh and it's keeping me pinned here."

Sourness filled Darby's mouth as she looked at the shattered dock. Wood in his leg. How big would the giant splinter be?

"I won't pull." Ann spoke soothingly, but her eyes were wide as she stared at Darby over Patrick's head.

"I'll just support you a little bit so that you can take some weight off your hands."

Ann crouched lower, but Patrick's arms kept trembling.

Darby wished she knew more about first aid. What she did know was that they were in big trouble and darkness was falling.

"Patrick, can I get underneath the dock?" Darby asked.

She didn't want to jump down and start poking around, wasting time, when Patrick knew every inch of this place.

"Not really." Patrick's pale face seemed to float above the rest of his body, but Darby heard him swallow and saw him make a shrug with one shoulder, as if he were trying to push his glasses up his nose.

Repositioning his glasses was something he did when he was trying to think.

Darby did it for him.

"What's the best way I can see your leg?" she asked.

"In that building where I keep tack, there's all kinds of stuff. A flashlight . . ." Patrick's voice trailed off.

"Do you think you're losing blood?" Ann managed. Darby couldn't see her friend's face. Ann was bent forward, and the position of her frizzy red hair made Darby think Ann's mouth was near Patrick's ear.

"At first I was afraid I'd cut my femoral artery. That big one in your thigh that gushes." He gave a shaky laugh. "But that wasn't it. Else I would have bled out already. So that's good."

"You've got that right," Ann said, and it was lucky Patrick couldn't see her expression of horror.

"So, really, I don't know how important it is for you to go look—" Patrick gasped as the shoe he had braced on the dock shook and his knee wagged to one side. He might have impaled his leg even worse if Ann hadn't held him tighter.

Once more, it was a good thing Patrick couldn't see Ann's face, or he would have known what the effort had cost her.

For a moment, fury replaced Darby's fear. Why wasn't someone here to help them? When would some adult arrive? Two eighth-grade girls couldn't be expected to handle a life-threatening situation on their own, could they?

"Hey, Patrick"—Darby tried to sound calm—"since you know about femoral arteries and stuff, I think you should help us out. Give the orders, you know?"

Darby knew her own look was panicked as she met Ann's eyes, but her friend nodded in instant agreement.

"Good idea," Patrick said. "I'm shocky already— you can tell by my clammy skin and stuff—but talking will help me focus. Uh, I think you're supposed to keep me warm."

Beads of sweat looked sickly silver on his pale face, but Darby had read enough adventure stories to know he was right.

"I can go get my saddle blanket and cover you, if Darby can hold you up?" Ann suggested. She must have shifted just a little in anticipation of doing that, because Patrick gasped in pain. "I'm sorry."

Patrick shook his head and began muttering. His voice went up and down as if he were really saying something, but the girls couldn't understand.

He really could be bleeding. Hemorrhaging. He could lose consciousness.

"I think I'd better go under as far as I can with a flashlight and see if you're bleeding. I can't remember what the third B of the three B's of first aid are, but you're breathing, and bleeding comes next," Darby insisted. "Can you hold him long enough for me to go find the flashlight in the shed and try to crawl under there?" she asked Ann.

Ann nodded.

"Why didn't you answer?" Patrick yelped.

"I nodded," Ann said. "Don't be so paranoid, buddy."

Even though she sounded jovial, Ann's face was just as pale as Patrick's.

Paranoid. She'd used the same term with her mother. Darby wished as hard as she could that this was the day they were supposed to go riding and her mother was on her way.

Ann mouthed the word *hurry* to Darby.

"I'll be right back."

Darby let herself hang by her hands off the edge of the dock for a second, then dropped to the ground.

Her mind pounded as her feet ran. Mistwalker trotted alongside her, frantic with worry. The other horses whinnied in puzzled distress. But the horses were all safe. Darby had to focus on Patrick.

Why wasn't someone—Jonah, Cade, Kimo, anyone on a fast horse, or in a truck—coming to see where they were? And now that she thought about it, too late, Mom *had* said she'd come ride on Tuesday. Today was Tuesday. Today had just felt like Monday because she'd missed the first school day of the week.

So her mother really might be on her way. She could help. One of her part-time jobs had been as a clinical aide at an elementary school. That was sort of like a nurse, so she could help. Or she could *go* for help. Call the hospital in Hapuna, maybe.

It would just make everything better if her mom were here.

Out of breath, Darby stopped in the doorway of the old building. Twilight was falling and the structure predated electricity, so she couldn't see much inside.

Looking for a flashlight in the dark was an example of irony Miss Day would love, but Darby didn't waste time enjoying it herself.

There! A red cross on a white box indicated a first-aid kit. She grabbed it, muttering, "Good thinking, Patrick."

For all that the kid said he was just a risk taker,

he knew he was accident prone, and since he spent so much time out here . . .

A snort came from behind her and Darby whirled to face Mistwalker. The paint looked like a jigsaw puzzle of a horse. Her splotches of white shone and her black parts became part of the darkening forest behind her.

Even though the horse had stopped neighing, she was nowhere near calm. Her eyes rolled and she tossed her head. She didn't look quite sane. She acted as if she might charge, forcing Darby to do something.

"Hey, girl, what do you think?" Darby was trying to soothe the horse, when she caught the glint of a metal flashlight. She grabbed it, switched it on, and sighed.

Don't congratulate yourself yet, Darby's brain ordered. She swung the beam around, looking for anything that could help them out of this mess.

Big metal wheels, ropes coiled on the ground, chains and tools hung on the wall. Shovels, rakes, a scary-looking sickle, wrenches of every size, a small hatchet . . .

Get going, her brain demanded. *Anything that will help is in that first-aid kit.*

But something held her here.

Sorry, Ann, she sent her friend a mental message. There was something about that hatchet. It was small, the kind you used with one hand. But it was hanging way up on the wall, beyond her reach.

"Darby?" a voice quavered through the rain forest. When she couldn't tell if it was Ann or Patrick, she knew she had to rush.

"Coming!" she bellowed.

She tried jumping up high enough to knock the hatchet off its hook. She tried three times before she thought of Mistwalker.

Jonah had trained her, and he always said he wanted a horse that would swim him to the mainland if he asked it to.

"You don't have to swim me to the mainland, girl," Darby said.

She grabbed a lock of the mare's variegated mane, clucked, and led her forward, as if there were no doubt in her mind Mistwalker would come along. Then, before the mare changed her mind, Darby vaulted onto her bare back.

Darby mumbled sweet nonsense to the horse. She stretched her aching arm as high as she could, and batted at the hatchet.

It came loose. Darby ducked out of the way and let it fall to the ground. She felt Mistwalker gather herself to buck.

She slipped off, and though the mare's startled squeal made the other horses whinny again, Darby didn't have time to comfort them.

"You're okay, Navigator, Soda," she called as Mistwalker galloped away. Her chest felt tight as she added, "I've got the first-aid kit, Patrick!"

She ran as fast as she could, but the hatchet was too heavy to carry and too clumsy to drag, so she alternated, and its metal head made furrows in the forest floor.

She was breathless, but almost back to the dock when another idea struck her.

Navigator had earned his name by knowing his way home from anywhere. If the big gelding galloped home riderless, Jonah would come.

"I'll be right back!" Darby yelled.

Despite Ann's sound of disbelief, Darby dropped everything and ran to the horses.

"You're okay," she told the worried geldings. "Navigator's going for help."

Darby jerked the quick-release knot loose, but the coffee-colored Quarter Horse just stared at her.

"Go home, 'Gator!"

Darby gave his rump a slap so that he knew he was free, and the gelding bolted into the rain forest, crashing through vines and over saplings instead of taking the trail.

Darby could only hope the horse knew a shortcut to 'Iolani Ranch.

As soon as she was in earshot, Ann said, "You have to get up here and switch places with me."

Ann must be desperate. Until now, she'd hidden her distress from Patrick.

Darby felt herself start to hyperventilate, except

that she couldn't. Her asthma-scarred lungs wouldn't allow it.

She closed her eyes and, oddly, thought of Hoku. She was trying to train her horse to face fear by lifting her head, stopping, and thinking. Not running around in circles or panicking.

Darby decided she'd better do the same thing.

She dropped the hatchet, pinned the first-aid kit under one arm, and swarmed up to join the others on the dock. It swayed under her assault and Darby heard Patrick moan.

She felt grateful for the sound and tried not to think too much about what *that* meant.

Of course Patrick was still alive. Brilliant eighth-grade boys didn't die in the jungle while they were playing pirate. It wouldn't be right.

Holding her breath, Darby took Ann's place. She placed her hands exactly where Ann's had been.

Shouldn't Patrick's shirt be damp with sweat? It wasn't.

"I'm really thirsty," he began.

"I have a canteen," Ann said, flexing her fingers before she picked up the flashlight.

"You can't give me water. I was just saying . . ." Patrick's tongue swept over his lips, but they didn't shine with moisture. "In case I have to have surgery," he explained.

Darby stared into the dark woods. Surgery seemed a long way off.

"I turned Navigator loose. He'll go home and everyone will know we need help," she said. Then she told them about getting the days mixed up. "I was supposed to go ride with my mother, and if I know her, she's got Jonah totally freaked out by now. She'll know exactly where to look for us. They're riding this way. I'm sure of it," Darby insisted. "And if Tutu sees Navigator first, we're still in good shape."

No one commented that "good shape" might be an exaggeration, but she felt them thinking it.

"I don't think there's anything creepy under the dock," Patrick said faintly. "Maybe you should see if you can look at my leg, because it doesn't hurt anymore. It just feels heavy. I didn't sever the artery or we'd probably see blood squirting, but if you could feel my pedal pulse; that's on my foot—"

Ann cut him off. "Patrick, I never thought I'd say this, but it's possible you know too much for your own good. You rest. I'll go look."

She hopped off the dock to do just that.

"Don't touch it, though," Patrick called weakly. "A broken bone could still cut that femoral artery after all. Wouldn't that be stupid?"

"Way stupid," Darby said. She closed her eyes, listening to Ann's movements. The dock was like a big wooden box, roughly rectangular, and though it might be open on the ends and worn with age and weather in places, she heard Ann grunt as she squeezed under the dock right underneath them.

It was quiet for a long time.

"I don't see any blood," Ann mumbled, and then there was a scuffing sound in the dirt.

"What are you doing?" Darby demanded.

"Scooting out backward from under the dock, like a badger or something. But there's no blood. None. Just that sliver going into Patrick's leg."

"Is it big?" Patrick asked.

"Boy, is it big," Ann said.

Darby winced at her friend's tactless response, but Patrick wanted yet more detail.

"Big like a Popsicle stick?" he asked.

"Big like . . ." Ann paused, and Darby's mind spun along with her friend's. "Smaller than your forearm." Ann's voice drew closer. "More like one of those stakes builders put in the ground when they're laying out a lot for a house."

Ann pulled herself back up. As she did, she tilted her head and mouthed incomprehensible words.

Darby shrugged, and Patrick's weight hung so heavy on her hands, she didn't have the energy to figure out Ann's charade.

Darby thought her wrist and elbow bones were pulling apart. She remembered thinking Patrick was heavier than he looked when she boosted him into Mistwalker's saddle.

He didn't feel so frail now, either. In fact, he seemed to be growing heavier.

"We still haven't done anything with the first-aid kit," Darby said. "Patrick?"

Darby looked down and Ann focused the flashlight on Patrick's wrist.

It reminded her of the white part of a celery stalk, just as pale and no bigger. Still, his pulse bumped blue and steady beneath the skin. He was either sleeping or unconscious, and that must mean he was getting worse.

She didn't want to use the hatchet, but she had to do it.

"Ann, listen. Step one: We cut the hole around his leg a little bigger. Step two: We sever the splinter at its base. Step three: We lift him out."

"Thank goodness," Ann said, nodding at the ground. "I thought, well, you know . . ."

Horror choked Darby.

Had Ann thought she wanted to cut off Patrick's leg?

"No. No! But we have to make sure Patrick's conscious and understands while we explain, because that would not be a good sight to wake up to."

Ann giggled.

"You're sick," Darby said.

"Hysterical, I think," Ann said, but she helped Darby awaken Patrick and explain.

"Flawless, it's not," Patrick said, "but it's a pretty good plan for now."

"Thank you," Darby said, and she and Ann began

using the flashlight to study Patrick's leg and the wood around it.

"Are you calculating angles?" Patrick asked.

"Of course," Ann snapped, but her hand covered her lips in dread.

Switching places with Darby, Ann held Patrick up while he trained the flashlight beam on his leg and the space around it.

To Darby, it appeared the wood was such a tight fit, it had actually peeled back a sheath of skin and left the meaty part of Patrick's leg exposed and open to infection.

She didn't mention that to Patrick or Ann. They had grim imaginations of their own. Besides, there wasn't anything she could do until she got her friend loose.

"Anyone else would tell me to be careful," Darby said once she had the hatchet up on the dock, but before she knelt to cut.

She hefted the ax's weight for a moment, checking for pain in her arm, but she didn't feel a single twinge of weakness.

"I just think you're brave to try it," Patrick said.

Brave? She was more afraid than she'd ever been. And what he'd said wasn't exactly a vote of confidence.

Once more, Darby reviewed what she was going to do. She couldn't cut too deep or she would injure Patrick with the blade, by ramming the splinter deeper or by creating a deadly trapdoor.

She held her breath, raised the hatchet, and suddenly the spot she was aiming for went black.

"Hold the light steady!" Darby screeched.

"Sorry!" Ann yelled back, but it wasn't her fault.

Patrick didn't say anything, but he was looking away, into the forest.

"Oh my gosh." Darby gasped. She'd almost brought the sharp blade down without seeing where it would cut.

"I heard something," Patrick said.

"I thought I did, too," Ann said, but her tone was as remorseful as Darby's was terrified.

"This time," Darby said, raising the hatchet once more, "Patrick, can you count for me?"

He held the light steady and began the countdown.

"One," Patrick said, in a steady voice. "Two."

And then all three of them looked away from the tiny vortex of light.

Hooves thudded on the rain-forest floor. A horse nickered and a voice called, "Stop, honey. It's Mommy, and I want you to put the hatchet down."

Chapter Sixteen

Ten minutes later, Jonah and Ellen, smelling of horse sweat and wind, helped the girls extract Patrick's trapped leg from the dock.

After surveying the boy's situation and talking to Darby and Ann, they widened the crack in the dock and sliced off the splinter at its base, just as Darby had planned. Then, they pulled Patrick straight up and out.

They didn't try to move him to the forest floor. Instead, they lay Patrick down on his back on the dock with Jonah's jacket folded beneath his feet. They cleaned the wound and pushed the skin back down where it belonged.

"That needs to be cleaned up by an expert," Ellen told Patrick.

It was no time for laughing, but Darby couldn't help being amused by Patrick's expression as he listened to her mom. Ever since Ellen had explained to him that his leg had been "degloved" by the old wood, introducing him to a term he'd never heard before, Patrick found her mother fascinating.

He stayed still as Ellen used every inch of gauze in the first-aid kit to wrap the injury and steady the splinter in place.

"We shouldn't pull it out? You're sure?" Ann asked. She studied the whole arrangement skeptically.

In the moment of quiet, horses squealed and neighed below them.

"I'm sure," Ellen said. "That's a job for a doctor in Hapuna. Or one of the EMTs on the ambulance."

Darby sighed, feeling weak with relief, because Jonah had explained that Aunty Cathy had called for help as soon as they saw Navigator gallop into the ranch yard.

"I am so glad I was right about where you were," Ellen said.

"Of course, a spirit horse led her here," Jonah joked.

"It did?" Darby asked.

Anything seemed possible in this forest of clouds and mist, but Jonah was only teasing.

And he was teasing her mother. His daughter. Some might not call that progress, but Darby did.

She thought of the quote Miss Day had written on

the classroom whiteboard: "Love isn't what you say, it's what you do."

Regardless of what Jonah said, he and her mom had ridden out here together. They were working side by side to help Patrick, and they'd both complimented Ann and Darby on the care they'd taken of their friend.

"I don't know how you could have missed that horse," Ellen said in frustration to her father.

"There was no horse but Navigator," Jonah told them in a loud whisper.

"Mistwalker," Ellen explained to the kids. "She was just off to the side of the trail the whole way here. Your horse loves you."

Patrick smiled without opening his eyes.

"You can ride her anytime you want," Patrick said. "I don't think she'll be getting much exercise from me. I'd feel a lot better if someone looked out for her." His eyes opened and for the first time all day, Patrick looked agitated. "What you said about keeping her safe—"

"I'll be around to help her out," Ellen said, smoothing Patrick's dark hair away from his sweaty brow. "Don't worry."

She would? Darby thought. Had Jonah and her mother worked out their problems? Or was Ellen just humoring Patrick to keep him quiet until the ambulance arrived?

Ann was staring at Patrick's leg, and the color in

her face was leaching away. Ann was paler than Darby had ever seen her. Now that everything was under the control of someone else, her friend looked as if she were about to faint.

"Ann," Jonah said, and the red-haired girl's head snapped up to look at him. "Could you go down and catch all the horses and tie them up? When we got here, we just trusted to their training, but when the ambulance shows up, there'll be quite an uproar."

"I will. I'll do it right now," Ann said. "Thanks."

In the quiet that followed, Darby felt as if she were about to cry. Her emotions were in a knot and she couldn't untangle them.

It began to rain, and as her mom rearranged the saddle blankets they'd placed over Patrick, she glanced down.

"There she is, Jonah," Ellen whispered. She pointed below them at Mistwalker.

Surrounded by ferns, the beautiful mare would have been invisible if it hadn't been for her white markings. The light that Ellen aimed from the flashlight made Mistwalker look like a magical woodland beast.

"Isn't she beautiful?" Darby said, squeezing her grandfather's arm.

Even someone who didn't admire paint horses had to see that Mistwalker was amazing.

When he still didn't say anything, her mom insisted, "You see her now, don't you?"

Jonah cleared his throat.

"Sure," he said.

"She's the horse you sold me," Patrick managed.

Ellen rested a hand on the boy's chest to keep him from sitting up, but she was also staring at her father.

"The paint," Jonah said to Patrick, but there was a question in his voice that even he heard. He cleared his throat again. "The truth is, I've got old eyes. I don't see so well in low light." He gestured at the trees and darkness. "My peripheral vision's not the best, either."

All at once Darby thought of Jonah squinting at her mom across the cremellos' corral, even though the sun was at his back. And the way he'd almost over-looked Ellen when he'd come to tell Darby to feed the pigs.

Oh my gosh, and the day of the earthquake! She couldn't figure out why he'd asked Aunty Cathy how bad her head injury was, but he might not have been able to see it very well. And one day he'd had Kit examining Black Lava's tracks when he could clearly see them himself.

Wait.

Darby felt a surge of sickness and concern. None of those things had taken place in poor light.

"How long has this been going on?" her mom asked. "This is what Cathy wanted you to tell me, isn't it?"

Jonah laughed and looked down at Patrick as if

it were guys against the girls. "Yeah, that's it, but you tell people you have a little — what do you kids say? — *issue*, and they're all over you. I don't need sympathy. I know my work better than most."

"Of course you do!" Darby said, but how bad would Jonah's eye condition get? Could it have anything to do with him always looking around for someone to take over the ranch after him?

"How long have you had it?" her mother insisted.

"Awhile," Jonah admitted with a wave of his hand. "Your mother," he said to Darby, who knew how much he hated being fussed over. He shook his head. "Let's discuss this later, yeah?"

"No," Ellen said evenly. "I won't stop asking, and since I can't ask Patrick to step out of the room, I'm going to ask for his discretion."

Patrick gave a nod.

"Give it up, girl," Jonah said. "I was a terrible father, but it was a lifetime ago."

"Were you worried about your eyes way back then? When Mama was alive?" Ellen's voice sounded suddenly girlish, and Darby's heart squeezed in sympathy.

Jonah pointed a finger at his daughter. "I'll tell you, but then that's the end of it, yeah? Not another word."

"Okay," Ellen agreed.

"At first I was pretty mad, yeah? Newly married and finding out there's this hereditary condition that could blind me. *Could*, you hear. It's not a sure thing."

Jonah lifted his chin before going on. "I kept it to myself because people are always remindin' me of it even without knowing. They say 'you won't believe your eyes,' and 'right before your very eyes' or 'even a blind man could see. . . .'"

Ellen hugged Jonah, leaning across Patrick to do it.

"And that's why you kept me in a cage when I was a teenager?" Mom demanded against his cheek. "You were afraid you'd need to see something and I wouldn't be there to be your eyes." She held him until he made a disgusted snort and wrenched himself free of her arms.

"Partly," he said, then smoothed one side of his mustache and winked as if his next words were a joke. "Are you gonna make me admit I didn't want to lose you, too?"

It was no joke and they all knew it.

"Look," Jonah said forcefully, "this disease? It's gone real slow. It's likely to keep on that way or maybe even stop. And I swear on my ancestors' bones, if either of you change—you, coming back home to take care of the old man," he said, pointing at Ellen, "or you, thinking I won't see when you pet my horses," he said to Darby, "forget about it.

"What kinda paniolo goes blind? I been thinking about it, and it seems to me, lately, he's the kind who sees people he loves a little more clearly. Now that's enough. Hear that siren? That snail of an ambulance is almost here."

According to what Tutu said later, Ellen and Jonah had done their own *ho'oponopono*. Darby wasn't sure she'd call it that. The reconciliation had begun when her mother said to Jonah, "Well, at least you had a reason to act crazy."

Still, Tutu credited Darby with forging a truce, if not peace, between her mother and grandfather.

Whether it was reconciliation, truce, or simple love, the next morning, before daylight, before Ellen's plane returned her to Tahiti, she, Darby, and Jonah were driven over to Sugar Sands Cove Resort by Kit to retrieve the herd of cremello horses.

Darby looked out the back window at the horse trailer. She could just glimpse the black-and-white face, and the sorrel one, inside.

It was thanks to the truce—and Patrick—that Ellen had gotten her way, Darby thought, smiling.

Patrick had sounded just like his usual self when he'd called from the hospital.

"My leg's not broken, thanks to all of you, but I'm on 'infection watch' for forty-eight hours, and after that, riding may be out of the question for some time," he'd told Darby. Then he'd begged her to coax Ellen into riding Mistwalker at least once before she left.

Ellen didn't need much coaxing. She'd called Patrick back with her promise, then started working on Jonah.

"No one has to know you bred her," Ellen had promised, and Jonah gave in.

Getting him to bring Hoku along, too, had been a bit more difficult. Why should they trailer two extra horses halfway across the island when they already had plenty to ride and some to herd in front of them? he'd demanded.

But Ellen had won. She and Darby were fidgeting with excitement by the time they reached Sugar Sands.

Aunt Babe wore mango-colored lipstick and a long dress that fluttered like a sheik's robe, even though none of her guests were out of bed yet.

"This is a good decision," she said.

"I made it weeks ago. You know that," Jonah grumbled as he backed Mistwalker out of the truck.

"You won't be sorry," Aunt Babe added.

When she moved close enough to pet the paint mare, Darby couldn't imagine why Mistwalker didn't shy at Aunt Babe's billowing garments.

"Don't gloat," Jonah said.

He shifted the saddle on Mistwalker's back. Since Patrick had been riding her both bareback and with an endurance saddle, the paint was equally comfortable with either. Then, Jonah handed Ellen the mare's black leather reins, watching to make sure the horse he'd trained still behaved. But he stood farther off as Darby coaxed Hoku out.

"You're amazing," Darby whispered to her filly. Even though Hoku's ears flicked in all directions, she'd actually backed into a strange situation without protest.

Darby wasn't the only one who noticed. She saw Kit nod and give her a thumbs-up before he got back into the truck. He looked out the driver's window and said, "I want to get on ahead of you all, so I can see the picture you make, driving the horses home."

Darby's heart was soaring and she was so amazingly happy, she almost missed the conversation between Jonah and her mother.

"What made you decide to take them?" Ellen asked as she petted the mare's satiny neck.

"Money," Jonah said gruffly, watching Kit drive away, as if that were more interesting than their talk. "I want these cremellos on the place before summer, to start earning their keep carrying my sister's tourists."

"Of course, they'll do that for you," Babe said, but Darby thought her great-aunt was studying Jonah as if she knew there was more to his decision.

"I'm socking away some money to build another house on the place," Jonah admitted.

Another house! Darby couldn't believe it! That could only mean that she and her mom and Hoku—

"Don't count your chickens before they hatch, Jonah," Ellen cautioned him, but she was smiling when she turned to hold Darby by the shoulders. "We're still working things out, your grandfather and I."

"Sure," Darby said, nodding wildly. "Of course. I won't count my chickens, either."

"However, if everything goes as planned—and you know—Darby, look at me."

She did, widening her eyes.

"You know, with Hollywood, that's a huge *if*. But I'm planning for us to live in Hawaii for the next two years."

"Or longer," Jonah said, winking at Darby as he saddled the tallest cremello.

"He's impossible," her mother said, and when she threw her hands up in mock despair, Hoku shied. "Sorry."

"No big deal," Darby said, but she'd bet no one understood her, because she was talking through the world's biggest smile.

Her cheeks hurt even after she'd pulled herself up on Hoku's sleek sorrel back.

When Jonah was mounted, too, Mistwalker put on a show of eagerness to be off—with or without her rider.

"You used to know how to do this!" Jonah said when the paint shied as Ellen reached for a stirrup with her borrowed boot.

Darby looked anxiously at her mother, but her mother was grinning, too, taking Jonah's words for teasing.

And once she was settled and sitting up straight and graceful, Ellen rode Mistwalker right up to Jonah's cremello mount, caught her father's face in gentle hands, and gave him a kiss on each cheek.

"I used to know how to do a lot of things," she said. "Now it's time to see if I remember."

And then they were off before Jonah could say a word in response.

Tropical wind pulled Darby's black ponytail out behind her. She smelled sea salt, greenery, and the glossy horses they herded toward 'Iolani Ranch.

Darby's heart sang as Hoku loped between her mother and grandfather, and Darby remembered the words Patrick had written on his cast.

Darby leaned into her filly's golden mane and whispered, "This is what I was born for."

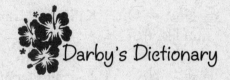

Darby's Dictionary

In case anybody reads this besides me, which it's too late to tell you not to do if you've gotten this far, I know this isn't a real dictionary. For one thing, it's not all correct, because I'm just adding things as I hear them. Besides, this dictionary is just to help me remember. Even though I'm pretty self-conscious about pronouncing Hawaiian words, it seems to me if I live here (and since I'm part Hawaiian), I should at least try to say things right.

ali'i — AH LEE EE — royalty, but it includes chiefs besides queens and kings and people like that

'aumakua — OW MA KOO AH — these are family guardians from ancient times. I think ancestors are supposed to come back and look out for their family members. Our *'aumakua* are owls and Megan's is a sea turtle.

chicken skin — goose bumps

da kine — DAH KYNE — "that sort of thing" or "stuff like that"

hanai — HA NYE E — a foster or adopted child, like Cade is Jonah's, but I don't know if it's permanent

haole — HOW LEE — a foreigner, especially a white person. I get called that, or *hapa* (half) *haole*, even though I'm part Hawaiian.

hapa — HA PAW — half

hewa-hewa — HEE VAH HEE VAH — crazy

hiapo — HIGH AH PO — a firstborn child, like me, and it's apparently tradition for grandparents, if they feel like it, to just take *hiapo* to raise!

hoku — HO COO — star

holoholo — HOE LOW HOW LOW — a pleasure trip that could be a walk, a ride, a sail, etc.

<u>honu</u> — HO NEW — sea turtle

<u>ho'oponopono</u> — HOE POE NO POE NO — this is a problem-solving process. It's sort of cool, because it's a native Hawaiian way of talking out problems.

<u>'iolani</u> — EE OH LAWN EE — this is a hawk that brings messages from the gods, but Jonah has it painted on his trucks as an owl bursting through the clouds

<u>ipo</u> — EE POE — sweetheart, actually short for *ku'uipo*

<u>kanaka</u> — KAH NAW KAH — man

<u>kapu</u> — KAH POO — forbidden, a taboo

<u>keiki</u> — KAY KEY — really, when I first heard this, I thought it sounded like a little cake! I usually hear it meaning a kid, or a child, but Megan says it can mean a calf or colt or almost any kind of young thing.

<u>kupuna</u> — COOI POO NAW — an ancestor, but it can mean a grandparent too

<u>lanai</u> — LAH NA E — this is like a balcony or veranda. Sun House's is more like a long balcony with a view of the pastures.

lau hala — LA OO HA LA — some kind of leaf in shades of brown, used to make paniolo hats like Cade's. I guess they're really expensive.

lei — LAY E — necklace of flowers. I thought they were pronounced LAY, but Hawaiians add another sound. I also thought leis were sappy touristy things, but getting one is a real honor, from the right people.

lei niho palaoa — LAY NEEHO PAH LAHOAH —necklace made for old-time Hawaiian royalty from braids of their own hair. It's totally *kapu*—forbidden—for anyone else to wear it.

luna — LOU NUH — a boss or top guy, like Jonah's stallion

mahalo — MAW HA LOW — thank you

malihini — MUH LEE HEE NEE — stranger or newcomer

menehune — MEN AY WHO NAY — little people

ohia — OH HE UH — a tree like the one next to Hoku's corral

pali — PAW LEE — cliffs

<u>paniolo</u> — PAW NEE OH LOW — cowboy or cow-girl

<u>pau</u> — POW — finished, like Kimo is always asking, "You *pau*?" to see if I'm done working with Hoku or shoveling up after the horses

<u>Pele</u> — PAY LAY — the volcano goddess. Red is her color. She's destructive with fire, but creative because she molds lava into new land. She's easily offended if you mess with things sacred to her, like the ohia tree, lehua flowers, 'ohelo berries, and the wild horse herd on Two Sisters.

<u>pueo</u> — POO AY OH — an owl, our family guardian. The very coolest thing is that one lives in the tree next to Hoku's corral.

<u>pupule</u> — POO POO LAY — crazy

<u>tutu</u> — TOO TOO — great-grandmother

<u>wahine</u> — WAH HE NEE — a lady (or women)

Darby's Diary

<u>Ellen Kealoha Carter</u>—my mom, and since she's responsible for me being in Hawaii, I'm putting her first. Also, I miss her. My mom is a beautiful and talented actress, but she hasn't had her big break yet. Her job in Tahiti might be it, which is sort of ironic because she's playing a Hawaiian for the first time and she swore she'd never return to Hawaii. And here I am. I get the feeling she had huge fights with her dad, Jonah, but she doesn't hate Hawaii.

<u>Cade</u>—fifteen or so, he's Jonah's adopted son. Jonah's been teaching him all about being a paniolo. I thought he was Hawaiian, but when he took off his hat he had blond hair—in a braid! Like old-time vaqueros—

weird! He doesn't go to school, just takes his classes by correspondence through the mail. He wears this poncho that's almost black it's such a dark green, and he blends in with the forest. Kind of creepy the way he just appears out there. Not counting Kit, Cade might be the best rider on the ranch.

Hoku kicked him in the chest. I wish she hadn't. He told me that his stepfather beat him all the time.

Cathy Kato—forty or so? She's the ranch manager and, really, the only one who seems to manage Jonah. She's Megan's mom and the widow of a paniolo, Ben. She has messy blond-brown hair to her chin, and she's a good cook, but she doesn't think so. It's like she's just pulling herself back together after Ben's death.

I get the feeling she used to do something with advertising or public relations on the mainland.

Jonah Kaniela Kealoha—my grandfather could fill this whole notebook. Basically, though, he's harsh/nice, serious/funny, full of legends and stories about magic, but real down-to-earth. He's amazing with horses, which is why they call him the Horse Charmer. He's not that tall, maybe 5'8", with black hair that's getting gray, and one of his fingers is still kinked where it was broken by a teacher because he spoke Hawaiian in class! I don't like his "don't touch the horses unless they're working for you" theory, but it totally works. I need to figure out why.

<u>Kimo</u>—he's so nice! I guess he's about twenty-five, Hawaiian, and he's just this sturdy, square, friendly guy. He drives in every morning from his house over by Crimson Vale, and even though he's late a lot, I've never seen anyone work so hard.

<u>Kit Ely</u>—the ranch foreman, the boss, next to Jonah. He's Sam's friend Jake's brother and a real buckaroo. He's about 5'10" with black hair. He's half Shoshone, but he could be mistaken for Hawaiian, if he wasn't always promising to whip up a batch of Nevada chili and stuff like that. And he wears a totally un-Hawaiian leather string with brown-streaked turquoise stones around his neck. He got to be foreman through his rodeo friend Pani (Ben's buddy). Kit's left wrist got pulverized in a rodeo fall. He's still amazing with horses, though.

<u>Cricket</u>—is Kit's girlfriend! Her hair's usually up in a messy bun and she wears glasses. She drives a ratty old truck and said, to his face, "I'm nobody's girl, Ely." He just laughed. She works at the feed store and is an expert for the animal rescue in Hapuna.

<u>Megan Kato</u>—Cathy's fifteen-year-old daughter, a super athlete with long reddish-black hair. She's beautiful and popular and I doubt she'd be my friend if we just met at school. Maybe, though, because she's

nice at heart. She half makes fun of Hawaiian legends, then turns around and acts really serious about them. Her Hawaiian name is Mekana.

The Zinks—they live on the land next to Jonah. They have barbed-wire fences and their name doesn't sound Hawaiian, but that's all I know.

Wow, I met Patrick and now I know lots more about the Zinks. Like, the rain forest—the part where Tutu told me not to go—used to be part of the A-Z (Acosta and Zink!) sugar plantation and it had a village and factory and train tracks. But in 1890, when it was going strong, people didn't care that much about the environment, and they really wrecked it, so now Patrick's parents are trying to let the forest take it back over. They hope it will go back to the way it was before people got there. I still don't know his parents' names, but I think Patrick said his dad mostly fishes and his mom is writing a history of the old plantation.

Oh, and that part Tutu said about the old sugar plantation being kind of dangerous? It REALLY is!

Patrick Zink—is geeky, super-smart, and seriously accident-prone. He looks a little like Harry Potter would if he wore Band-Aids and Ace bandages and had skinned knees and elbows. He says he was born for adventure and knows all about the rain forest and loves Mistwalker, his horse. He's not into his family being rich, just feels like they have a lot to pay back to the island for what their family's old sugar cane plantation did to it environmentally. He likes it (and so do I!) that they're letting the rain forest reclaim it.

<u>Tutu</u>—my great-grandmother. She lives out in the rain forest like a medicine woman or something, and she looks like my mom will when she's old. She has a pet owl.

<u>Aunt Babe Borden</u>—Jonah's sister, so she's really my great-aunt. She owns half of the family land, which is divided by a border that runs between the Two Sisters. Aunt Babe and Jonah don't get along, and though she's fashionable and caters to rich people at her resort, she and her brother are identically stubborn. Aunt Babe pretends to be all business, but she loves her cremello horses and I think she likes having me and Hoku around.

<u>Duxelles Borden</u>—if you lined up all the people on Hawaii and asked me to pick out one NOT related to me, it would be Duxelles, but it turns out she's my cousin. Tall (I come up to her shoulders), strong, and with this metallic blond hair, she's popular despite being a bully. She lives with Aunt Babe while her mom travels with her dad, who's a world-class kayaker. About the only thing Duxelles and I have in common is we're both swimmers. Oh, and I gave her a nickname—Duckie.

<u>Potter family</u>—Ann, plus her two little brothers Toby and Buck, their parents, Ramona and Ed, and lots of horses for their riding therapy program. I like them all. Sugarfoot scares me a little, though.

<u>Manny</u>—Cade's Hawaiian stepfather pretends to be a taro farmer in Crimson Vale, but he sells ancient artifacts from the caves, and takes shots at wild horses. When Cade was little, Manny used him to rob caves and beat him up whenever he felt like it.

<u>Dee</u>—Cade's mom. She's tall and strong-looking (with blond hair like his), but too weak to keep Manny from beating Cade. Her slogan must be "you don't know what it's like to be a single mom," because Cade repeats it every time he talks about her. My mom's single and she'd never let anyone break my jaw!

<u>Tyson</u>—this kid in my Ecology class who wears a hooded gray sweatshirt all the time, like he's hiding his identity and he should. He's a sarcastic bully. All he's really done to me personally is call me a *haole* crab (really rude) and warn me against saying anything bad about Pele. Like I would! But I've heard rumors that he mugs tourists when they go "off-limits." Really, he acts like HIS culture (anything Hawaiian) is off-limits to everyone but him.

<u>Shan Stonerow</u>—according to Sam Forster, he once

owned Hoku and his way of training horses was to "show them who's boss."

<u>My teachers</u>—
Mr. Silva—with his lab coat and long gray hair, he looks like he should teach wizardry instead of Ecology
Miss Day—my English and P.E. teacher. She is great, understanding, smart, and I have no idea how she tolerates team-teaching with Coach R.
Mrs. Martindale—my Creative Writing teacher is not as much of a witch as some people think.
Coach Roffmore—stocky with a gray crew cut, he was probably an athlete when he was young, but now he just has a rough attitude. Except to his star swimmer, my sweet cousin Duckie. I have him for Algebra and P.E., and he bugs me to be on the swim team.

❧ ANIMALS! ❧

<u>Hoku</u>—my wonderful sorrel filly! She's about two and a half years old, a full sister to the Phantom, and boy, does she show it! She's fierce (hates men) but smart, and a one-girl (ME!) horse for sure. She is definitely a herd girl, and when it comes to choosing between me and other horses, it's a real toss-up. Not that I blame her. She's run free for a long time, and I don't want to take away what makes her special.

She loves hay, but she's really HEAD-SHY due to Shan Stonerow's early "training," which, according to Sam, was beating her.

Hoku means "star." Her dam is Princess Kitty, but her sire is a mustang named Smoke and he's mustang all the way back to a "white renegade with murder in his eye" (Mrs. Allen).

<u>Navigator</u>—my riding horse is a big, heavy Quarter Horse that reminds me of a knight's charger. He has Three Bars breeding (that's a big deal), but when he picked me, Jonah let him keep me! He's black with rusty rings around his eyes and a rusty muzzle. (Even though he looks black, the proper description is brown, they tell me.) He can find his way home from any place on the island. He's sweet, but no pushover. Just when I think he's sort of a safety net for my beginning riding skills, he tests me.

Joker — Cade's Appaloosa gelding is gray splattered with black spots and has a black mane and tail. He climbs like a mountain goat and always looks like he's having a good time. I think he and Cade have a history; maybe Jonah took them in together?

Biscuit — buckskin gelding, one of Ben's horses, a dependable cow pony. Kit rides him a lot.

Hula Girl — chestnut cutter

Blue Ginger — blue roan mare with tan foal

Honolulu Lulu — bay mare

Tail Afire (Koko) — fudge brown mare with silver mane and tail

Blue Moon — Blue Ginger's baby

Moonfire — Tail Afire's baby

Black Cat — Lady Wong's black foal

Luna Dancer — Hula Girl's bay baby

Honolulu Half Moon

Conch — grulla cow pony, gelding, needs work. Megan

rides him sometimes.

<u>Kona</u>—big gray, Jonah's cow horse

<u>Luna</u>—beautiful, full-maned bay stallion is king of 'Iolani Ranch. He and Jonah seem to have a bond.

<u>Lady Wong</u>—dappled gray mare and Kona's dam. Her current foal is Black Cat.

<u>Australian shepherds</u>—pack of five: Bart, Jack, Jill, Peach, and Sass

<u>Pipsqueak/Pip</u>—little shaggy white dog that runs with the big dogs, belongs to Megan and Cathy

<u>Tango</u>—Megan's once-wild rose roan mare. I think she and Hoku are going to be pals.

<u>Sugarfoot</u>—Ann Potter's horse is a beautiful Morab (half Morgan and half Arabian, she told me). He's a caramel-and-white paint with one white foot. He can't be used with "clients" at the Potters' because he's a chaser. Though Ann and her mother, Ramona, have pretty much schooled it out of him, he's still not quite trustworthy. If he ever chases me, I'm supposed to stand my ground, whoop, and holler. Hope I never have to do it!

Flight — this cremello mare belongs to Aunt Babe (she has a whole herd of cremellos) and nearly died of longing for her foal. She was a totally different horse — beautiful and spirited — once she got him back!

Stormbird — Flight's cream-colored (with a blush of palomino) foal with turquoise eyes has had an exciting life for a four-month-old. He's been shipwrecked, washed ashore, fended for himself, and rescued.

Medusa — Black Lava's lead mare — with the heart of a lion — just might be Kit's new horse.

Black Lava — stallion from Crimson Vale, and the wildest thing I've ever seen in my life! He just vibrates with it. He's always showing his teeth, flashing his eyes (one brown and one blue), rearing, and usually thorns and twigs are snarled in his mane and tail. He killed Kanaka Luna's sire and Jonah almost shot him for it. He gave him a second chance by cutting an X on the bottom of Black Lava's hoof wall, so he'd know if he came around again. Wouldn't you know he likes Hoku?

Soda — Ann's blue-black horse. Unlike Sugarfoot, he's a good therapy horse when he's had enough exercise.

Buckin' Baxter — blue roan in training as a cow horse and I can stay on him!

<u>Prettypaint</u>—used to be my mom's horse, but now she lives with Tutu. She's pale gray with bluish spots on her heels, and silky feathers on her fetlocks. She kneels for Tutu to get on and off, not like she's doing a trick, but as if she's carrying a queen.

<u>Mistwalker</u>—is Patrick's horse. She's a beautiful black-and-white paint—bred by Jonah! He could hardly stand to admit she was born on 'Iolani Ranch, which is silly. Her conformation is almost pure Quarter Horse and you can see that beyond her coloring. And what he doesn't know about Mistwalker's grandfather (probably) won't hurt him!

❧ PLACES ❧

<u>Lehua High School</u>—the school Megan and I go to. School colors are red and gold.

<u>Crimson Vale</u>—it's an amazing and magical place, and once I learn my way around, I bet I'll love it. It's like a maze, though. Here's what I know: From town you can go through the valley or take the ridge road—valley has lily pads, waterfalls, wild horses, and rainbows. The ridge route (Pali?) has sweeping turns that almost made me sick. There are black rock teeter-totter-looking things that are really ancient altars and a SUDDEN drop-off down to a white sand beach. Hawaiian royalty are supposedly buried in the cliffs.

<u>Moku Lio Hihiu</u>—Wild Horse Island, of course!

<u>Sky Mountain</u>—goes up to five thousand feet, sometimes snow-capped, sometimes called Mountain to the Sky by most of the older folks, and it's supposed to be the home of a white stallion named Snowfire.

<u>Two Sisters</u>—cone-shaped "mountains"—a borderline between them divides Babe's land from Jonah's, one of them is an active volcano.

<u>Sun House</u>—our family place. They call it plantation style, but it's like a sugar plantation, not a Southern mansion. It has an incredible lanai that overlooks pastures all the way to Mountain to the Sky and Two Sisters. Upstairs is this little apartment Jonah built for my mom, but she's never lived in it.

<u>Hapuna</u>—biggest town on island, has airport, flagpole, public and private schools, etc., palm trees, and coconut trees

<u>'Iolani Ranch</u>—our home ranch. 2,000 acres, the most beautiful place in the world.

<u>Pigtail Fault</u>—Near the active volcano. It looks more like a steam vent to me, but I'm no expert. According to Cade, it got its name because a poor wild pig ended

up head down in it and all you could see was his tail.
Too sad!

<u>Sugar Sands Cove Resort</u> — Aunt Babe and her polo-
player husband, Phillipe, own this resort on the island.
It has sparkling white buildings and beaches and
a four-star hotel. The most important thing to me is
that Sugar Sands Cove Resort has the perfect water-
schooling beach for me and Hoku.

<u>The Old Sugar Plantation</u> — Tutu says it's a dangerous
place. Really, it's just the ruins of A-Z sugar plantation, half of which belonged to Patrick's family. Now
it's mostly covered with moss and vines and ferns, but
you can still see what used to be train tracks, some
stone steps leading nowhere, a chimney, and rickety
wooden structures which are hard to identify.

❧ ON THE RANCH, THERE ARE ❧
PASTURES WITH NAMES LIKE:

<u>Sugar Mill and Upper Sugar Mill</u> — for cattle

<u>Two Sisters</u> — for young horses, one- and two-year-
olds they pretty much leave alone

<u>Flatland</u> — mares and foals

<u>Pearl Pasture</u> — borders the rain forest, mostly two-

and three-year-olds in training

<u>Borderlands</u> — saddle herd and Luna's compound

I guess I should also add me . . .

<u>Darby Leilani Kealoha Carter</u> — I love horses more than anything, but books come in second. I'm thirteen, and one-quarter Hawaiian, with blue eyes and black hair down to about the middle of my back. On a good day, my hair is my best feature. I'm still kind of skinny, but I don't look as sickly as I did before I moved here. I think Hawaii's curing my asthma. Fingers crossed. I have no idea what I did to land on Wild Horse Island, but I want to stay here forever.

DARBY'S GENEALOGY

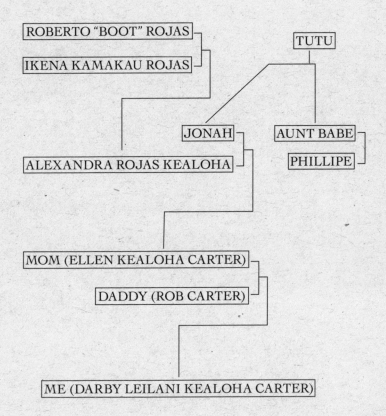

Darby and Hoku's adventures continue in . . .

WATER LILY

 Water Lily

Darby Carter lay belly down, as level to the ground as she could make herself. Her chin rested on red dirt. The grass of the Lehua High School football field tickled her nose, but everything about her remained still — except for her eyes. They tracked the wild horses' every step as they followed the early-morning sun.

Without raising her head, Darby could only see the black stallion from hooves to chest. He stood that close.

Darby's best friend, Ann Potter, lay beside her. Ann was supposed to be equally still and silent, and though her unruly red curls didn't move, Ann whispered an imitation of a documentary film narrator.

"While stalking the crafty colts of Wild Horse Island—"

"Shh." Darby tried not to smile.

"—two intrepid naturalists were unable to conceal themselves from a pack of slobbering sophomores, with the end result that they were trampled quite—"

"Ann!" Darby hissed. She elbowed her friend in the ribs, even though the black mustang hadn't bolted. "Shh."

They weren't stalking crafty colts, or concealing themselves from other students—sophomores or otherwise—but after two frustrating weeks, she and Ann had given up following the rules.

Fearing the stallion would charge some student, the parents, teachers, Mr. Nomi from the Department of Agriculture, and the school's principal, Ms. Cooke, had all been taking turns patrolling the horses' temporary pasture at the school to keep the kids away.

They'd been pretty good at it, too, Darby thought. Each time she and Ann had come out to the field to check on the wild horses they'd helped rescue from the tsunami waters, they were shooed away "for their own safety."

This morning they'd finally crept close enough to really watch the horses, because they'd persuaded Ann's dad to drop them off an hour before classes began.

Darby had expected it to be cold this early in the day, but it hadn't rained since the tsunami. The earth was drying out and felt almost warm beneath her. Sunshine heated the denim of her jeans, too, but Darby didn't close her eyes and bask.

Who knew when she'd get this close to the horses again? So she took in every detail of Black Lava, studying the sloping pasterns and wispy feathers on the black stallion's legs.

He could run forever, Darby thought. She sighed, and the stallion lowered his head to investigate. Equine eyes—one brown and one blue as her own—fixed on her.

"He's watching us." At Ann's voice, a bay mare gave a low nicker and moved farther away.

Eight horses remained in Black Lava's band. Before the tsunami, there'd been eleven.

Snorting, the night-black stallion moved far enough away that Darby saw all of him. Head high, he trotted a circle around his herd.

The stallion stopped beside a dun mare and lifted his muzzle as if pointing out the girls. He stood half a football field away, but Darby heard wind sing through his tail.

He and the dun sniffed, nostrils widened to take in the smell of the humans.

The horses had been forced to call this place home, but they didn't welcome visitors.

A squeal from one of the mares sent the herd off at a run, to the far side of the field. What had startled them?

Before Darby could roll up on her side to investigate, a voice told her it was a *who*, not a *what*.

"You don't mind standing up and coming with me, do you?" Ms. Cooke's question was really more of a command.

Darby closed her eyes. She knew they were caught but didn't want to face it.

"Girls?"

Darby and Ann pushed themselves onto their knees, then stood, brushing at the grass and dirt on their clothes as they looked at each other and tried to think of something to say.

"No surf this morning?" Ann asked finally.

"I could find bigger waves in my bathtub," the principal said scornfully.

Ms. Cooke was a world-class surfer. Most mornings she arrived at school with her sun-bleached hair still wet. But the moment she stashed her teal-blue surfboard behind her office door, Ms. Cooke turned into a no-nonsense principal.

"Let's go." Ms. Cooke strode off.

She clearly expected them to follow and, though excuses swirled through her mind, Darby couldn't find the nerve to say anything. She'd seen Ms. Cooke around campus, but they'd never met.

Ann was less intimidated by the principal. As the girls caught up with her, Ann pointed in the opposite direction. "Our first class is this way, Ms. Cooke."

Ms. Cooke gave them a smile that crinkled the skin

around her eyes. "We're headed for the office. You two knew the field was off-limits. You took a chance and lost."

"What's going to happen?" Darby knew she sounded chicken.

"A citation." Ms. Cooke's voice floated back to them as she continued walking. "And Nutrition Break detention for the rest of the week."

"A citation?" Darby gasped.

That was bad. Really bad. Short term, it might mean she couldn't ride out with her friend Cade to Crimson Vale today after school. Long term, it could be much worse.

One of her mother's ground rules for remaining in Hawaii and on 'Iolani Ranch, her grandfather's ranch, depended on Darby earning good grades. Of course that meant citizenship grades, too. Her mother said perfect behavior didn't take much brainpower.

Although Darby had only been in Hawaii for two and a half months, she'd already been in trouble more than she had during her entire life in Southern California.

Megan Kato, the daughter of the business manager on 'Iolani Ranch and one of her best friends, had told Darby it was because she was actually doing things — riding the grasslands of wild Hawaii, for a start — instead of sitting in her room reading.

Darby had used that explanation when her mother had visited last week. Her mother, Ellen Kealoha

Carter, was an actress. She was shooting a pilot for a TV series in Tahiti. Early reviews of the new series were great, and Ellen had said that since shooting time would be divided between Southern California and Tahiti, Darby's plea that the two of them live in Hawaii was a possibility.

Since Ellen had grown up on Wild Horse Island, she'd been somewhat understanding about Darby's adventures and mishaps.

But no excuse would do if a formal reprimand was placed in Darby's school file.

Darby's mind raced, searching for some way out of this. She concentrated on her honey-brown boots, moving in step with Ann's blue-gray ones as they crossed the campus behind the principal. Curious looks and a few laughs followed them.

She must have swallowed audibly as she got ready to negotiate with Ms. Cooke, because Ann gave a quick shake of her head. Her expression said things could be a lot worse, so Darby didn't protest. She just hurried to keep up.

The bell for first period was ringing when Darby and Ann finished signing their names to forms detailing their punishment. The girls were sprinting, hoping to get to class on time when Megan Kato waved her hand and shouted to get their attention from across the hall.

"Hey! You get to see the horses?"

"We did, but oh my gosh, Meggie, you'll never

guess what kind of trouble—"

Darby tugged at Ann's sleeve. Ann and Megan had been soccer teammates and were friends. If Ann stopped to explain, in her usual dramatic detail, they'd be tardy to English.

"We'll tell you at lunch, okay?" Darby said.

"Keep letting Crusher get you in trouble, and you'll make me look like the angel of the family," Megan said. She formed her fingers in a halo above her Cherry Coke–colored hair before hurrying toward her own class.

"Angel," Ann scoffed as they hurried on.

Darby hitched her backpack up higher and vowed she wouldn't let Megan's prediction come true.

Discover all the adventures on Wild Horse Island!